SWIMMERS

Published in Canada by Red Deer Press, 195 Allstate Parkway, Markham, Ontario L3R 4T8
Published in the United States by Red Deer Press, 311 Washington Street, Brighton,
Massachusetts 02135

10 9 8 7 6 5 4 3 2 1

Red Deer Press acknowledges with thanks the Canada Council for the Arts, and the Ontario
Arts Council for their support of our publishing program. We acknowledge the financial
support of the Government of Canada through the Canada Book Fund (CBF) for our
publishing activities.

**Canada Council
for the Arts**

**Conseil des Arts
du Canada**

ONTARIO ARTS COUNCIL
CONSEIL DES ARTS DE L'ONTARIO
an Ontario government agency
un organisme du gouvernement de l'Ontario

Library and Archives Canada Cataloguing in Publication
Bright, Amy, author
 Swimmers / Amy Bright.
Issued in print and electronic formats.
ISBN 978-0-88995-513-4 (pbk.).--ISBN 978-1-55244-332-3 (pdf).--
ISBN 978-1-55244-331-6 (epub)
    I. Title.
PS8603.R542S95 2014   jC813'.6   C2014-902881-4
                                               C2014-902882-2

Publisher Cataloging-in-Publication Data (U.S.)
Bright, Amy.
    Swimmers / Amy Bright.
[216] pages : cm.
Summary: After a tragic event in Victoria, 17-year-old Hunter escapes to Lethbridge, where
he is home-schooled with his neighbor, a young girl named Poppy. Hunter's girlfriend
Lee arrives in Lethbridge to take him back to confront his past, and all three make the bus
journey together.
Also available in electronic format.
ISBN-13: 978-0-88995-513-4 (pbk.)
1. Teenagers – Conduct of life – Juvenile fiction. 2. Teenagers – Substance use – Juvenile
fiction. I. Title
[Fic] dc23 PZ7.B75448Sw 2014

Edited for the Press by Kathy Stinson
Design by Daniel Choi
Cover image courtesy of iStock

Printed in Canada by Friesens Corporation

MIX
Paper from
responsible sources
FSC® C016245

SWIMMERS

Amy Bright

Red Deer Press

For my Mom and Dad, Robin and Glenn

On the Bus

The bus went over a bump in the road, making me fumble for my backpack. I leaned over the aisle to hand Poppy a can of Coke. She swatted it away.

"I'm not thirsty," she said, shoving her hands into her pockets.

"Suit yourself."

I handed it to Lee instead. She cracked the top and Coke fizzed out all over her hand. I shrugged a sorry. It's not my fault the bus driver was hitting all the major bumps. Minor potholes between here and Victoria shaking up the soda.

We were on a Greyhound bus, skinny and metallic, on our way from Alberta to British Columbia. Poppy shouldn't be on this trip but she was—twelve and pissed off. I had a stab of panic in my chest just thinking about what it meant that she was here. Lee, seventeen like me, sat beside her, sophisticated ponytail swinging like a metronome.

Outside the window was a blur of coulee, prairie, coulee.

Tall grass. Flat highway. It was going to take one whole day to get home. Twenty-seven hours sitting on a bus, and then a ferry ride, still on the bus, and then one more spurt into the city.

Three months ago, when I did this trip in reverse— Victoria to Lethbridge—it had taken only half of that. Fourteen hours. That's how fast Mom and Dad wanted me out of Victoria and moving in with Aunt Lynne in this tiny Alberta city I'd never even been to before. Dad drove me to Lethbridge at the beginning of the fall. Early September, shorts and T-shirt weather, and us trapped in his tiny car with the windows rolled up tight. *Sans* flip-flops, swimsuits, and beach towels. Now it was almost Christmas and I was going back.

I hadn't been on a bus that first time. I rode shotgun in Dad's Ford Focus, the engine a little pissed about all of the mountain passes it had to make it through.

Dad as a travel buddy was a whole lot different from Lee and Poppy. Poppy was sitting in the seat opposite, listening to the music on my iPhone. I hoped she didn't find the Fuck Yeah songs. I kept forgetting she wasn't even in high school, not even close.

In an unbelievable turn of events, Lee was holding my hand. We were sweating hard between our palms, half because I didn't think either of us was expecting this, and half because the bus driver had the heat cranked. Poppy checked out our hands between the seats. I tried to remember what, if anything, I'd told her about Lee while we sat at that big table in her Mom's kitchen being homeschooled. Probably nothing. Hopefully nothing.

"Hey, Pops," I said, because she was side-eyeing the hell out of us. "How are you doing for snacks?"

Her left eyebrow jerked halfway up her forehead.

"Snacks?" she asked, making fun of the way I'd said it.

"Yeah," I said. "Snacks."

"I'm okay," she said. She could make her voice sound so small. Maybe it was her on-the-bus voice, lowered a few decibels out in public company. She didn't sound that way in real life. I had spent the last three months with her, and I still didn't get how she could stick herself to me like glue, but no one else. She was even a little suspicious of Lee.

Watching them get on the bus together that morning had given me major secondhand embarrassment. The two of them standing in an aisle, two seats to the left, two to the right, trying to figure out where to sit. They ended up on opposite sides, Poppy on the right window, Lee on the left. It was my job to play musical chairs between them. But that tension was good. It gave me something else to think about besides Niall. He was on a repeating loop on the inside of my head. The reason I was going home.

I kept hearing this stupid song in my head. Something that was big on the radio that summer when me and Niall really started hanging, a catchy indie hit. I'd snag myself on a snippet of that song and I'd go right back to thinking about Niall again. What we were going to find when we got to Victoria.

"That music okay?" I asked Poppy. "It's not too poppy for you?" I smiled at my joke.

"Yeah," she said. "It's fine. And I've heard that one before. Probably about a million times."

"It never gets old," I said.

"Trust me," Poppy said. "It does."

I don't know why it felt good to have her along for the ride, but it did. We were like a professional wrestling tag team, high-fiving support back and forth to each other. Right now we were up against the ropes. But we still had time to make a comeback. The BC border was still miles away. The island even farther.

"I think we can stop to get something to eat later," I said. We hadn't had time to grab breakfast. Poppy had been waiting for me on her front steps at 8 AM. Her mom had left early and had no clue that Poppy was gone. I was scared about that. I'd taken Poppy with us without telling anyone.

I asked Lee if she had raided the minibar last night, but she kindly reminded me that run-down motels do not have much on offer. Zip and zilch. She'd stayed at one down the street from Aunt Lynne's house, so that we could all leave together on the bus the next morning.

"Me and my Dad stopped at a Subway when we were a couple of hours away from Aunt Lynne's house," I said. "I think it was in Banff. We're stopping there next. If I'm not mistaken," I added, twirling my invisible moustache because the real one wasn't in yet. I wanted to crack Poppy up. Make her less mad at me. Try to worry less about what was going to happen when her mom figured out she was gone.

"Hey, Pops," I said, trying one more time. "You okay?"

"I'm fine."

"She's okay," Lee said and gave my hand a little squeeze. Lee had come to Alberta to bring me back home. No one else knew I was coming. When we talked on the phone, me in Lethbridge, my parents in Victoria, I wasn't allowed to ask about Niall. I wasn't allowed to ask if they'd been to the hospital. I wasn't allowed to ask if they'd heard anything. We just talked about Aunt Lynne and me and how we were doing.

Fine, fine, fine.

Bzzzzzzz. "Hunter Ryan to the office, please. Hunter Ryan."

The first day I heard my name on the intercom, I noticed it slid in between Hailey Pearlman and her arms all cut up from these safety scissors she stole from art class, and Nolan Leder with his Dad's new girlfriend, who had the son who handed out black eyes before breakfast. I knew things had gotten pretty bad, because the only way you got to talk to Penner was if you had a referral. I was going through everybody I could think of on my slow walk to the office, trying to figure out who had pointed the finger. Teachers, parents, students. Anyone could've said something.

Mr. Penner might have taught high school psychology but that didn't make him a psychologist. There were a grand total of zero diplomas hanging up in his office. Still, the school board thought it was a good idea to set him up in a room by the atrium once a week on Fridays. All day you would hear the intercom calling kids to the office to talk to Penner about some bullshit reason why they couldn't get to class on time in the mornings.

I shuffle-stepped into Penner's office while the secretary was watering the potted plants. She spritzed them with a spray bottle. Short, short, long.

"Hunter," Penner said. He was balding on top. You had to hand it to him for not letting the hair he did have grow into a ratty ponytail. He kept it neatly cut. His nose looked like it had come out of the prosthetics department for *The Hobbit*, and his gums showed too much when he smiled. For a guy who stuck out as much as that, it was the first time I could remember ever seeing him at Douglas High, just another one of Victoria, BC's ordinary public high schools.

"One of your teachers recommended I see you," he said.

"Just the one?" I asked.

Penner shuffled a few papers on his desk. "Your name has been brought to my attention a few times."

At the time, I would've bet you it was Saunders or Kesler, Math and Bio, respectively. They hated my guts. But I found out later it was Saunders and Kesler, all my other teachers, and a couple of friends who had put the word out that I needed help. The whole school was out for me.

"So, what do I have to do?" I asked him.

"Well, we'll meet here for half an hour every Friday and talk. Get a sense of what's going on in your life. I just want to know what's going through your head."

Half an hour was nothing for Penner. He used the session to introduce himself. I learned he didn't have a lot going on outside of the school. He was a retired guy, called back in to talk to students and look like he was being useful. That first session, he told me I'd do the talking. The way he saw it, I was a big set of wooden doors just waiting to open. At the end of the half-hour, he smiled and shook my hand.

Nolan walked into Penner's office when I was leaving. He was staring at the ground with his face all beat up and those bruises aging badly. I had seen his stepbrother around. He was six foot two. Nolan didn't have a chance.

One night that week, my sister Bridget stayed after dinner. She sat on the couch and watched TV with Mom and Dad. At the end of the night, she went upstairs and fell asleep in her old bedroom, even though she had an apartment downtown. She sold used books at the bookstore two streets away from her place, the famous one that was always getting written up about in the newspaper. I didn't know why she'd want to be home, sharing a bathroom with yours truly.

Her bedroom door was closed tight in the morning, and I heard her hair dryer on high while she got ready for work. I didn't want to meet her down in the kitchen and hang around while we waited for the toaster to pop. Instead, I grabbed my backpack and went outside, and there was my stomach growling away, telling me to get back in there and grab a bowl of cereal, cover blown before I even left the house.

The cement was grayer than gray. It rained all night and, surprise, high school started first period at the crack of dawn. It was only a ten-minute walk from our house to Douglas High School. There was no way to finagle a ride out of Mom and Dad when school was just around the corner.

The school sat in the middle of a square lot of land. It was treeless around the building and the school was on one level, low to the ground. I was early. The halls were empty and I could've missed the rush, but I shoved myself into the bathroom anyway and carved out a wide buffer.

The door was missing from one of the two stalls in the bathroom. I picked the other one, the one with the busted lock, sat on the toilet and held the door in place with my foot. No one used the bathrooms behind the gym. I knew that because me and Niall had used this bathroom to smoke weed in the afternoon last semester, in between Social and Math. Niall would prop open the window and push the screen. Niall was a goddamn tree, he was so tall. We'd smoke his neatly rolled joints close to the window, me sitting on the edge of the sink and Niall leaning against the wall.

No one talked about Niall anymore. He wasn't at school, which meant people stopped thinking about him. Think about how hard it is to try to continuously remember everyone you've ever known. To care enough to keep them as more than just a snapshot in your head.

Niall had dark hair and eyes and his clothes hung loose and ill-fitting. He had a nose that you noticed the way you do when you see two people kiss in the movies, when they slide side by side instead of crashing into each other. The big Niall thing, the one that kept him golden even when everyone started turning on him, was that he was like no one else. Try finding that in someone you know. You always look at a person and then compare them to what you know about everyone around you. You couldn't do that with Niall.

Sometimes that was hard on him. Sometimes he just wanted to be like everyone else.

One night last year, he came over for dinner and he was on something, his eyes all big and planet-like. Dad had been stirring something on the stove before he came over. We were talking about him. Me telling them he was my friend from school, Bridget making fun of me.

"Got a boyfriend, Hunter?" Bridget asked, raising her eyebrows.

"Get lost."

"Is that why he's coming over for dinner?" Mom asked, and I glared a hole right in the side of Bridget's head.

"No, Mom."

"Right," Bridget said, hip-checking me into the counter. "Because he's got a girlfriend. Lee." She drew out the eeeee's.

"Lee's not my girlfriend," I said, feeling my face turn red.

"She is so," Bridget said.

Dad just stirred the pot in an easy, even way. He wore a lot of plaid shirts and jeans, and Mom ran around on errands in some of those shirts, oversized and swimming.

I leaned on the counter and drank a glass of water. Mom and Bridget made the conversation a one-two punch.

"Have you met him?" Bridget asked Mom.

"Who?"

"Neil."

"Niall," I said.

"Yeah, Niall. Have you met him?" Bridget asked.

"Not yet," Mom said.

"Dude," Bridget turned to me, "think about how much that hurts his feelings. Don't keep your boyfriend a secret."

"He is not. My boyfriend."

"Bridget," Dad said. "We don't know all of your friends."

"Yeah, you do, Dad."

When Niall got there, I thought I was the only one who could tell that he had this eye thing going on. The entire time I knew him, he was always on something. He didn't like the way things were when they weren't blurred around the edges, stretched out and slow.

I didn't blame him. Niall and his family, it hadn't been easy for them.

I answered the door alone. For a few seconds, it was just the two of us on the porch. The outside lights were all on. Niall's eyes filled his face, and I was mad at him for doing that with my family around.

"It's okay. I'm fine," he told me.

He answered their questions at dinner. Every single thing they threw at him. I kept busy by looking around the table. The placemats were the striped ones, four long lines ending in corners. The lights on, the dark outside, the chairs all used up.

After dinner, we went into the living room. Bridget turned on the TV but went to her bedroom almost immediately after. Mom and Dad sat on the couch, Dad with his magazine and Mom with her laptop. Me and Niall sat on the floor and watched whatever was on. Niall swayed back and forth. Twice he was lucky the edge of the couch kept him from falling over.

Living in Victoria made you really familiar with the ocean. Out on the beach, I was always looking at the way the moon reflected on its surface, that big yellow globe staring right back at me from the water. I used to look at that and know there was no way I was going to strain my neck and look up into the sky to see the real thing. Not when it was staring up at me from the water.

I guess what I'm saying is that Niall was that full moon, the real sky moon. Not some reflection. And you made a point of looking up.

Sitting in the bathroom stall, lock all busted up, I wished I had some weed to take the edge off of first period, but that was Niall being gone and me too much of a loser to find someone else to smoke up with. I kicked at the door. With my foot back on the floor, there was nothing to hold it open and it folded inward, open to the rest of the empty bathroom.

I checked myself out in the mirror before I went to class. Bridge had been using my shower when I woke up, so I skipped having one of my own. My hair was all greasy, but it was dark enough that you couldn't tell. What do I know? Of course you could tell. You look around a high school and you know exactly who isn't showering and who doesn't wash their clothes and who has to skip breakfast in the morning.

There was a zit on my chin, small enough that if I left it alone, it would go away by itself. Bridge used to freak me out about them. "Pop it or it'll seriously just lurk around forever," she always told me. I knew I wasn't going to turn out to be one of those guys that all the girls want. I knew when that magical period of growing out of bad looks and baby fat was over. I was on the other side and knew what I was stuck with. I gave myself a look, eyebrows raised, and headed to Kesler's class.

Penner, who pretended to be cool with me at first, had gone into psych mode by our second meeting.

"I've been up-front about this, Hunter," Penner said. "This is only going to work if you talk to me."

"Penner," I said, "what is it exactly that you want me to tell you?"

He looked at his paper, like maybe the answer was written there, the point of our half-hour Fridays.

"Okay, let's try this, Hunter." I smiled and cringed, trying to help him notice his pattern of first-name-basis. "Why don't you tell me a little about your family?"

"Sure," I said. It was always the easy stuff first. "My mom teaches yoga downtown and Dad's a lawyer. They're pretty lax about his hours. He's home a lot. Bridget's my sister."

"And?" Penner asked. "Where's your descriptive sentence about her?"

"Bridge is Bridge," I said.

Penner laughed. Thought I was funny as shit.

"You've got a good family. I remember your sister. She was smart."

"Yeah, well, you never had to live with her."

Penner looked down at his papers to check and see where we were going next.

"How about your friends? Who do you hang around with outside of school?"

He clammed me up pretty good with that one. It was weird when old people used hang as a verb. He had his hands folded together and resting under his chin, waiting for some more of my comedy gold. If I told him the truth, I knew I'd be seeing him for a while. He just had to take one look around the school to see that I wasn't hanging around with anyone. I shot for the middle.

"I guess I hung out with Niall Black."

Penner looked at me in a whole new light. There he was, finally figuring out why I was here.

"You were friends?"

"Kind of," I told him.

Niall had been in high school with me since Grade 9, but I didn't notice him until the first day of Grade 10. I noticed him because, one day in class, he looked like he was dying. Of all those long-term diseases that make people just waste away, it looked like Niall had gotten the shit end of at least five of them.

He was acting weird at school that day. I watched him dig a hole in his desk with an unsharpened pencil all through last period. It was journey-to-the-center-of-the-earth style, the way a drill looks when it's moving in the ground. Niall was making some serious headway into the center of his desk, and it was sketchy as shit.

When the bell rang, Niall didn't move. He held onto

the edges of his desk like he was trapped there, the four sides growing high and making a box around him. He was sweating. Fat drops of that stuff were falling on his papers. Mrs. Brook watched him carefully. Niall kept gripping the edges of the desk, really white-knuckling them, until I walked over and said, "Niall, Mrs. Brook is going to get you in a lot of shit if you don't stand up right now and walk out of the classroom with me."

It was the first time I'd ever talked to him, after a whole year of passing him in the hall. He looked right through me. His eyes were spacey and gone, but he stood up, long legs awkward and odd.

"Hey, you can lean if you want," I told him, "because you're not looking too good."

"Yeah," Niall said, holding onto my arm with a vice-grip. "Yeah, thanks."

We walked out of the classroom and into the hallway, his fingernails digging into my arm.

"Hunter, is everything okay?" Mrs. Brook asked, shouting from her classroom.

"Yeah, we're fine."

Niall had zombie legs. Those tent-pole legs. I got the feeling he was all loose change, barely holding it together.

When we got out of the school, I leaned Niall against the side of the building and adjusted my backpack, the straps over my shoulders. There was a skinny line of school buses parked in front of the school.

"Look, do you need to get a bus or something?" I asked him.

"I'm not going home yet."

"Yeah, well, I think it might be a good idea if you did."

"I know I look bad," he said. "I was going to walk home. If you want to come, that would be cool."

"Yeah?"

"It's twenty minutes. We can cut through the woods."

Niall started walking. He didn't check to see if I was following, but I was. He brushed his hands against his pockets, trying to find where they opened and, when he removed them, he was holding a couple of pills. They weren't circle-shaped. These ones had edges that made them into tiny pentagons.

"You want one?" he asked.

"What is it?"

Niall tossed one into his mouth and set one right down in the middle of my hand. I didn't drink, hadn't even taken a sip of beer from some uncle at Christmas, but I took a pill from Niall, something that looked messy.

"It's prescription," Niall said. "It's fine."

"You take this stuff a lot?" I asked him.

Niall shrugged. It was the biggest "yes" I'd ever seen.

I didn't know the woods enough to cut through them. They're all over the place in Victoria, these little pockets of trees growing together frantically, afraid of the future development that could mess with their routine. Niall seemed to be okay. We moved from the rocks and dirt to a narrow path that looked to run the whole way through.

"What are we supposed to do now?" I asked.

"What do you want to do?"

"I don't know."

I could feel it a little. Right there.

Niall sat down twice, and the difference between sitting and standing was enormous. When we found the wall, we were almost on the other side of all the trees. Niall climbed on top and sat with his feet dangling down. I climbed up beside him. The cracks we used as footholds were filled with green moss.

When we came out on the other side of the woods, Niall put his arm out to stop me from going any further. A row of houses sat in front of us, spread far apart because of their acre yards, their iron fences, their circular driveways.

"It's probably better if you don't come in," Niall told me. "Maybe another time."

"Oh," I said. He looked like he needed someone to check up on him. This close to passing out on the grass.

"My parents are home," Niall said. "They're not so big on company."

It was another month before I was finally let into that house. Niall's parents stayed on the top floor and didn't come downstairs for anything. I found out they were a mess because Niall had a sister who had died in Vancouver. Her pictures were all over the house, on mantelpieces and bookshelves. Niall never looked at them for too long. He walked through his house with blinders on, eyes on the carpet in front of him.

"Was it hard? What happened?" Penner asked, snapping me back into that office, slingshot-style.

"I guess," I said.

"You guess?" He asked the question with a smile, which meant he didn't expect me to answer. "Okay, Hunter," he said, repeating my name like a mantra. "We're done for today. But we'll talk about your friends again next week, especially Niall. You think we can do that?"

"Sure."

He watched me leave.

I bumped into Lee when I was leaving his office, slamming right into her, yellow hoodie, jeans, legs and all.

"Hey, careful, okay?" Lee said.

I backed away, shrugging my shoulders at her.

"Jesus, Hunter," she said, when I didn't say anything. Guess I was all glued up from my talk with Penner. "Say sorry, at least."

"Sorry," I said. I looked at her then. A crease formed between her eyes, deep and pronounced, but she wasn't pissed off.

"Yeah, well, watch where you're going," she said.

For a second, it was just us, standing in front of the secretary's desk. What I told Penner was true. I hung out with Niall. But before Niall, before I noticed him sitting at that desk, there was Lee.

She leaned over the counter to talk to the secretary. She was on her tiptoes, even though she was tall enough to see over. I took one more look at her yellow hoodie before I headed out the glass doors and went back to class.

On the Bus

Me, Poppy, and Lee were all bundled up and clinging to the shoddy heat being filtered through the bus. The Greyhound was only a quarter of the way full, if that. Either it wasn't a popular time to be traveling through the Rockies, or else Greyhound had suffered a major setback.

I had been sharing a pair of headphones with Lee and, when she leaned away from me to look out the window, the headphones yanked out of my phone and flooded our section of the bus with Drake. An older woman sitting directly in front of us whipped her head around so fast, showing off her hyena-glare. She pursed her lips, an aging case of duck face, probably puzzling out why the three of us were traveling together. After that, she kept taking micro-turns in her seat whenever we were too noisy, catching me in the corner of her eye and holding me in one place.

Everyone on the bus was either a double or a single. I

could only see the tops of heads, and it did not tell you very much, that small amount of a person. Old or young, mostly, not much in between. White and gray or brown and blonde. Short and permed or long and styled. Not all of them were going to Victoria. There were about a dozen stops along the way. But I was curious about who would be left when we got all the way west, as far as you could go.

And it made me wonder who was going to be waiting for me on the other side, welcoming me back home. It was a multiple-choice game with no right answer: a) Mom, b) Dad, c) Bridget, or d) None of the above.

Or it could be surprise answer e) Mr. Penner. I'd had a couple of months with him when I still had to go to school, between what happened to Niall and leaving Victoria.

Homeschooling with Poppy in Lethbridge was cool. It was the first thing I'd felt good about in a while. No bells. No intercom. No announcements in the morning. Just a table and a bowl of snacks, with Poppy's mom stacking paper and handing out pencils. Me working on my Grade 11 work and Poppy working on Grade 7.

When I remembered the direction the bus was headed in, my stomach punched my lungs, heart, and kidneys some quick one-twos. It was asking: What do you want to go back for? But then there was Lee's hand holding on tight and the mountains signaling the slow climb home, and Poppy at the window, bobbing her head with the music from Lee's phone, and I tried hard to make myself feel normal.

When the bus pulled up to the station in Banff, we had ten minutes to stretch our legs. Banff looked like BC, with those mountains and fir trees laden with snow. It was blizzarding at the top of the mountain; you could see it swirling when you tipped your head back.

When me and Bridge were still in single-digit ages, Dad took us skiing. The whole time, I remember being cold and wet. Cold from the weather, wet from falling down every time I tried to pizza-slice turn. But I also remembered the way it felt when you were that high up the mountain and the fog suddenly fell beneath you. Instead of looking up at it, it was down below you, under your skis. You knew you'd have to tip forward and swish and slide through it to get to the bottom.

"So, how are we going to do this?" Lee asked. We were third from the front of the line at Subway, scanning the menu on the wall. "Split them or have our own?"

I shrugged, the one-thousandth one this trip. My shoulders just took to it naturally. Up and down. No words necessary.

I had these moments when I knew exactly what the right decision was. Leaving Victoria. Leaving Lethbridge to go back. But then I had these moments where things just happened because I was checked-out enough not to give a shit about what happened next. Checked-out like Niall had been.

Poppy was here with me and Lee because I'd checked out a couple of seconds too early, and told her to stuff a few clothes in her backpack, and lifted the straps over her shoulder before I checked in again. I knew I couldn't take a kid away from home and expect to get away scot-free. It didn't matter how much she'd wanted to come or how much I wanted her here. She tied me to something that finally felt like normal, and I didn't want to give that up. Not yet.

Lee and Poppy worked out what they were ordering, keeping me out of it. I backed out of the line and headed into the men's room. I washed my hands, Lady Macbeth-style, and knew I should try to pee because I'd seen what the washroom looked like on the Greyhound, and it was basically an upscale porta-potty. But I couldn't make a move from the sink. I just turned the heat up higher on the tap, the cold extinguished completely. My hands turned pink and then red, and I held them under and watched them soak it up. The bus route was a game of tug-of-war that I lost back in Alberta, and now I was being dragged forward all the way to the end.

The flaps of the pizza box were hanging off of my bed. Ham and cheese, Hawaiian minus the pineapple. Mom and Dad had left to go to a benefit dinner on the other side of the city, leaving me twenty bucks for an ordered-in dinner. Penner had given me about a dozen writing assignments to work on since our meetings started. He had sent me home with an assignment for the weekend. His half-hour sessions had started to leach into real life. Now he wanted me to write about my "friends."

The old piece-of-shit PC was taking up half the space in my bedroom. The only thing that worked was a word-processing program without spellcheck. Its ability to pick up an Internet connection was a crapshoot. I watched the cursor blink on the empty Word document for fifteen minutes, on and off, on and off.

The only place I could think to start was with Lee. The first sign of my world whirlpooling away was when Lee stopped hanging around. She saw what me and Niall did and she didn't like it. And I hated seeing her looking all disapproving and sad, so I sped things up a little and helped her see her way out.

Josh stuck around for a while. I'd known him since middle school. He was always over at Niall's, lying back on the couch with his feet on the coffee table, watching whatever was on TV and drinking cheap beer with both of us. It was luck of the draw whether he'd be there when Niall called me over. Most of the time he was, and I never could tell if that was lucky or not.

"Hunter," Josh said this one day, bobbing his head all friendly and dickish at me. "How's it going, man?" He was sitting on the couch in Niall's living room, smoking up and messing around with his cell phone. We were all skipping school together, three empty desks in Miss Pearson's English classroom.

"Where's Niall?"

"Kitchen," he said, jerking his thumb. "You in or out?"

"In."

Josh reached into his pocket and pulled out his tin of Altoids and, because I was still way too new, I figured I was getting a mint, something that was supposed to be all fresh breath and just-brushed teeth. He let me pick out a couple of pills, one of this kind, one of those, and shut it again with a little click.

"Hey," I said to Niall, finding him in the kitchen.

Niall was quiet, cracking open a beer and playing around on his computer. There's different kinds of friends, I guess, and Niall was the kind that you could just be easy and quiet around.

"Hey. You want to see something cool?"

Niall dragged his laptop across the counter, and we played music videos on YouTube over and over for the rest of the afternoon. He knew all of the stories, the why they were made, the who they were funded by, the what they were about way down underneath. Josh stayed in the living room, the volume of the TV rising and lowering every couple of minutes. When I went over to Niall's house, it was never any more serious than taking a couple of pills or smoking up, or drinking a little beer and being normal together.

Sometimes Niall would pass out in the middle of the afternoon, slumping against the arm of the couch with his eyes shut tight. When that happened, me and Josh would turn him on his side, just in case he threw up, and leave the house quietly. Those were the only times I ever checked out the pictures on the mantelpiece, the ones of Niall's dead sister. I only took a second look when Niall couldn't see me doing it.

From the pictures, you could tell she had long black hair and dark brown eyes. I knew she was younger than Niall by a couple of years. Middle school, maybe. Eighth grade when she died. He never said how, just that it was the reason they moved to the island from Vancouver. It was his mystery, the dark unreadable center.

"He doesn't look good," Josh would say when we left Niall passed out at his house.

"He's fine." It was always my job to reassure.

Staring at the blinking cursor, I thought about that year a lot. Me, Josh, and Niall hanging around together and missing school. Now I didn't have Niall or Josh in my life.

I never got around to typing up an assignment for Penner. He'd be pissed when I showed up empty-handed at our next meeting, but I didn't care.

Most mornings that spring I was back in the bathroom stall at school, jamming my legs up against the metal door to keep it shut. Penner's next appointments were always sneaking up on me, even though I could bullshit most of it. But it turned out his homework assignments were messing with me a little. They made me take my problems home with me, lay them down on my bed, and unfold them like clean laundry.

One morning I was in the bathroom, waiting for the bell to ring between one Penner appointment and the next. I was in nowhere zone. I couldn't feel the toilet seat under me and my legs were tense from holding the door closed. I was waiting out the ten minutes before the bell, when the bathroom door flew open. It was all "mmmummshhh" siphoned in from the hallway, everybody's voices mixing together.

"Dude, you in here?"

It was Josh.

I got the feeling it was Penner's fault that he was there. Penner was making me think about people again. He was making me write some paragraph about Josh on a Saturday night, and then making him materialize back into my life.

"Yeah," I said and let the door swing open. My legs were pins and needles.

Josh was wearing his basketball jersey. He watched me look at the number, the school name on the front.

"You didn't come out to the last game," he said, tugging at his shoulder.

"Guess not."

"Whatever, man. Didn't think you would."

Somehow, Josh could do all the shit he did with me and Niall and still play basketball for the school on a weekly basis. It beat me how he did it, but he was pretty good.

I realized I was still sitting on the toilet, so I stood up and went to lean against the row of sinks. Josh checked himself out in the mirror.

"You ever think about him?" Josh asked me, his eyes not leaving his reflection in the mirror.

We didn't talk about it, me and Josh. The thing with Niall happened over the Christmas holidays. Josh visited him once in the hospital. I didn't.

"Sometimes," I said.

"Man, we haven't even talked about it. The way he looked when I saw him. Not like he was."

"I got class," I said, my hand on the door. That nauseous feeling was already in my chest, making me want to puke.

"Dude, hang on," Josh said, reaching into his pocket. It was like stepping back in time, Josh and his Altoids container. His crooked smile giving it all away. "I got something for you."

"It's cool," I told him. "I'm fine."

"Nah, take this. It's on me." He held out two pills, pushed them into my palms. "Double or nothing."

I swallowed one dry and stuffed the other one into my pocket. It was routine. Don't ask questions; just take whatever's on offer. Niall taught me that from the very beginning, when we stood in the woods after I dragged him out of class and took him home. Even after what happened with Niall, I still played by his rules.

"Thanks."

"Hey, it's no problem. Glad you're back to being the old Hunter I remember." He barked out a laugh. "See you around."

That time, when Josh opened the door to the hallway, there wasn't any sound leaking back in.

He left me with my heart jumping around, back and forth in a warning. I stayed in the bathroom after he was gone, thinking back to before.

This one time last year, in Grade 10, Niall had gotten in a fight out in the high-school parking lot at lunch. Maybe if I'd been around, I would've been able to stop him from getting his ass kicked. I wasn't Mr. Tough Guy or anything, but I had thrown my fair share of punches. Even just roughhousing with Josh. It was all practice for the real thing.

But I wasn't around.

Niall got his ass handed to him. He had been knocked out cold for a solid fifteen minutes. Landed himself an appointment with the school nurse. Someone in the office had convinced him that he wouldn't be able to go back to class in his messed-up clothes. They were ripped-up and bloody. He couldn't sit at a neat plastic desk looking like he'd just climbed out of the cage at a UFC match. Someone pulled a pair of jeans and a T-shirt out of the Lost and Found and told him to make the switch. The Lost and Found was made up of clothes that were left in the gym change rooms overnight and collected by the janitors after hours. Most of it got claimed the morning after. Sometimes clothes got left for weeks. But the big rule was: you never took something that wasn't yours out of that Lost and Found.

Niall came back to class in a Lost and Found outfit.

We knew whose clothes they were. Joseph Clark's T-shirt, the college that his brother went to stamped on the front. Dark jeans with the patch on the left pocket that Trey Hudson had showed off when he bought them.

Everyone knew. Niall was rich as shit but, for that afternoon, kids teased him for being so messed-up he had to steal clothes from the Lost and Found. Didn't matter how much money he had, he couldn't erase how much they hated him that day.

It was Josh who got him sorted out at the end of the day, giving him a spare gym strip from his locker before basketball practice. Josh who made sure those borrowed clothes got back to the Lost and Found where they belonged.

Josh's spare pill was in my pocket. I checked it out and, when I held it up to the light, I found out it was a Tylenol. Nothing more than a little pain relief. I kicked the metal door hard, feeling vibrations in my heel. The last thing I was going to do was go back to class. So I went out into the empty hallway, but only to get to the front doors of the school.

If Penner was doing a summoning of Josh back into my life, then he had Lee going as a side project. She was sitting out on the lawn when I walked by. A couple of girls were sitting with her, doing this shitty little giggle, high-pitched with knives on. Full of the gifted Tylenol, nothing to even me out, I got out of there fast. Lee and me. Elementary, middle, high school. We went so far back.

Ten minutes later I was home. The driveway was empty. The house key was missing from my jacket pocket and I tipped out the contents of my backpack, searching for it. The doors were locked and there was no way to jack open a way in. I scooped everything back into my pack and left it leaning against the door, a kind of "Hunter Was Here," in case anyone came home at lunch and felt generous enough to leave a door unlocked for me. Being carless in Victoria wasn't a big deal. The buses went everywhere, and it didn't get cold enough to make walking impossible. I took the bus downtown and walked down to the wharf from there. Up Dallas Road where the cruise ships came in, big motherfuckers all lit up and on holiday.

There were a couple of places where you could get off the main road and head down the steps to get to the rocky beach. Mom always thought you could tell tourists from the locals based on how much time people spent staring out at the ocean. By her definition, I was a tourist, staring out there for hours. Just passing through.

On my way to school on Friday, I stopped outside of

Bridget's work and knocked on the window. She was helping a customer at the counter, but she still took a second to look for where the knock was coming from. I gave Bridge a small Queen Elizabeth II wave. She hadn't been around the house as much over the last week. She was sleeping at her apartment again, just dropping by the house for supper a couple of nights a week. There was no pattern to how much she came and went. She just did her own thing.

Friday mornings had turned into a holiday because of my meetings with Penner. I was missing a nice half-hour chunk of Biology once a week.

Someone else had been entered into the Penner rotation. I didn't know the guy, never even heard his name before, but he was called instead of Hailey Pearlman one morning, another replacement, another problem. I saw him coming out of Penner's office when I got to the secretary's desk. He was skinny as hell, his shirt hanging off of his chicken-wing arms, his loose jeans over toothpick legs. I had an urge to high-five him in solidarity.

"Hunter, how're we doing today?" Penner asked me when we were settled.

"We're good," I said, apparently answering for both of us.

"Do you have something for me?"

"Yeah, I typed something up," I told him, "but my computer crashed so, poof, I guess I don't have it today."

His eyebrows knit together. It was the second time I'd used that one.

"Should we switch to handwritten assignments from now

on? We can preempt a few of those technological issues that way."

"Nah, my dad'll have it fixed over the weekend."

Penner spent the next ten minutes in full-on silent treatment. He picked up a pile of papers and flipped through them. He made a couple of check marks and thick x's on them, turned them over and did the same thing to the other side. He made a phone call to some dude called Craig before he organized one of his desk drawers. I took it all in. I had nowhere else to be.

"Hunter," he said, eventually, "if you don't make time for me, what's the point in me making time for you?"

"The computer crashed. That's seriously it," I told him.

I could see Penner was exasperated. He wanted his hands around my neck so he could go full-on throttle.

"Is there a reason you don't want to tell me about your friends?"

"Uh, maybe because there isn't anything to tell you."

Penner raised an eyebrow. King of the expression, that guy was.

"I know Niall's story."

"Yeah, well, Niall's not here anymore."

"True, he's not at school. Have you ever thought of visiting him at the hospital?"

"No."

"This all seems very hard to deal with, Hunter."

"It's fine. I'm fine. I dealt with it."

Penner shook his head. "Something like this doesn't just go away on its own. It's only a few months since it happened.

That's not long."

"Three," I told him, before I remembered that I don't tell anyone anything.

"If I give you another writing assignment, can you complete it for next Friday?"

"Sure."

The intercom called the next person down—back to Nolan—and Penner pushed a piece of paper across the desk.

"Your assignment," he said.

I didn't look at it until I was in the hallway. Good thing. I might have thrown it right back across the desk at him, balled up grenade-size.

Write about your last day with Niall.

I knew what Penner meant by the last day. He meant during Christmas holidays when everything changed. No way in hell I was going to write about that.

I could have had a different last day with Niall months before, when I was given my first chance to bail on him. Maybe I could write about that.

We had gone to an end-of-class bash before the summer started. It was out on a stretch of private beach. Some rich bitch from school invited everyone over, BYOB. Me and Niall took the bus out there, and I figured we'd catch a ride back with someone sober enough to drive, or spend the night.

Niall was lit by the time we got there. I don't know what he took before the party. He didn't even touch a beer the entire night, so whatever it was kept him going all by itself. I kept an eye on him, only drinking a couple of beers. Lee wasn't at the party. She'd had a family thing and didn't feel like making the trip up the coast, just far enough away from her place that it was an inconvenience. I don't even remember Josh being there, which was uncharacteristic. Him missing a party. So there wasn't anything occupying my attention. I could keep track of Niall the entire night and not lose him for even a second.

We hung out in that giant house, eventually ending up in this piano room. A back-of-the-house sunroom with a baby grand and stacks of music. It was something my Aunt Lynne would've been jealous of. She had been a concert pianist.

"Dude, this is great," I told Niall. "Wish we had one of these at home."

Niall, who probably did have one of those at home—somewhere in his giant mansion—didn't say anything.

"You having a good time?" I asked him. "Feels good to be done school."

Niall shrugged his shoulders. I'd gotten used to the way he would shut right up when he'd taken too much of something. I slouched into a high-backed chair and closed my eyes. I thought I'd give us both a little silence.

So I did take my eyes off of Niall for a second. And that second was all it took for him to lose his fucking mind.

The crash exploded in the little room. I shot up from the chair and surveyed the place. He'd thrown the big piano bench through a window. The glass had broken mostly outward. Not cleanly, but it had made a big enough hole to get out of.

My ears ringing, I grabbed Niall by the arm. Pushing

him roughly through the opening, I said, "Get out." I leapt through after him, not looking back. I pushed him down into the bushes and then dragged him toward the front of the house. He wasn't helping. He was a dead weight. A gash ran along his forearm.

"Dude, you cut your arm." I hated him for getting caught on the glass. The opening was so large, he would've had to try hard to catch himself on the shards. His blood was on my hand, warm and sticky.

"You don't even feel it, do you?" I said. "You're so fucking numb from whatever you took, you don't even know you've got a fucking open wound. You don't even know you're bleeding all over the place."

Niall shrugged.

I turned away from him, my hands balled into fists. My fingernails were digging into my skin. "That is some crazy shit."

"Where are you going?" he asked. No change in his voice. Just flat, easy Niall.

"Home."

I started walking down the long driveway. I figured if I got out onto the main road, I'd be visible enough for a taxi to find me. I was already calling for one.

"Hunter." Niall called out from behind me.

"Leave me alone," I told him. "Find your own way back."

He caught up with me. I'd never seen that expression on his face before, this snarl that made him look inhuman. He shoved me, two hands to the center of my chest.

Niall lost his balance instead of me. Still, he came at me

again, this time with his fists instead of his open hands. I felt his knuckles hard on my cheekbone, heard a crack that shuddered through the side of my face.

I turned away from him and I eased into a run. He didn't come after me. At least, not fast enough to make it to the main road in time for the cab. It was idling by the stop sign. I held the door open, took one more look up the road behind me, and Niall was there, staggering all over the place. He suddenly seemed like more trouble than anyone I'd ever known. I had never cared less about what happened to him. I ducked into the cab.

I guess the guilt didn't really hit me until I'd been home for an hour or two. Lee hadn't texted and neither had Josh. I was alone in my bedroom and I couldn't get a hold of either of my best friends.

So I started texting Niall. Just to check in. Make sure he got home okay. He was suddenly the fallback guy again. The person I called when I had nobody else.

I figured the fight was a one-off. No one's himself, not completely, taking as many drugs as Niall did. So what if that meant he was hardly ever himself? At least I could count on him being there.

He didn't text back. I sent about a dozen texts throughout the night, finally passing out and sleeping until noon. There was still nothing from him.

I bussed over to his house. I'd been there a couple of times by that point, more than a couple. Niall opened the door when I rang the doorbell and let me inside. We went straight into the kitchen, where he had left a half-eaten bowl of cereal. While he spooned it into his mouth, I saw that he was wearing a hospital bracelet. His name typed out neatly, the date stamped underneath.

"When did you go to the hospital?" I asked him.

"Last night," he said.

"Why?"

He talked through a mouthful of cereal. "I passed out on someone's front lawn. They called an ambulance and I woke up at Vic General. Nothing happened. I'm fine."

We never said anything about that June night after that. And I never left him on his own again. I watched out for him like he watched out for me.

But I wasn't going to write about that in Penner's assignment, either. I bunched up the assignment and stuffed it into my back pocket. I walked through the school with my head down, trying not to think about anything.

"Hey, hey," Josh said, catching me in the hallway. He dropped his palm, open and heavy, on my back. It took the wind out of me. "How's the psych ward?"

I pushed past him.

"Dude, tell me you had a headache after that." He grinned, bringing up his pick-and-play Tylenol joke. I walked fast but he was faster.

"There's a party tomorrow night. Come by, yeah? I'll hook you up."

"Where?"

He shrugged, like it was no big deal. "Lee's."

"I'll think about it."

Nodding at Penner's office, the door still open, he said, "Watch your brain around that guy." He backed away down the hallway, holding onto his head and pretending he was getting an electric shock, his manufactured buzzing echoing down the hallway.

The night of the party, I took the bus to Lee's place in Oak Bay. I don't know how Josh convinced me it was a good idea, but I felt like I was doing the right thing.

It was going to be hard to get home if I stayed until the buses stopped running. I couldn't bank on getting a ride from anyone, especially not Josh, who would be blackout drunk by the time the party ended. And I couldn't trust some asshole who wanted to tell me he knew all about what had happened to Niall, when we were out in the middle of nowhere, heading in the wrong direction. Worst-case scenario was making the long trek on foot.

The trees were dark and thick. I tried to make out the house numbers, but they were covered by shadows that stretched long over neatly manicured lawns. A girl maybe my age was sitting ahead of me on the bus. I kept on taking these looks at her, hoping for some coincidental moment of her looking back at me at the same time. But that didn't happen. It doesn't happen. You sit on the bus in your own little world when you're traveling alone.

The bus had that soggy smell of winter turning into spring, when the rain and the fog sink into Victoria in April.

Wet boots, wet socks, wet jeans.

I could tell I was in Oak Bay when I saw the first big house with the big yard, and the gate pushing up against the sidewalk. I waited two more blocks before I pushed my hand against the yellow tab by the window, the "Stop Requested" scrolling above the driver's head. He pulled against the sidewalk and we parted ways.

Lee's house was my second home before Niall's was. I had a couple of dinners there a week, some pizzas ordered in from delivery, and Chinese food that arrived in folded boxes and Styrofoam containers. Josh would be there sometimes, but mostly it was just me and Lee. It was a lot to give up, when I chose to be friends with Niall over everyone else.

I walked up the six cement steps to the solid, wood front door. I thought for a second that I should ring the doorbell and give her a heads-up that I was coming, but it was a party and that wasn't what you were supposed to do. I pressed down on the door handle and pushed my way in.

Lee's house could fit four of mine inside of it, all wrapped up like a present. A staircase met you at the front door. It led up to the second floor where the bedrooms were, a second living room, the exercise room, and the washrooms. It was the hands-off-don't-even-think-about-going-up-that-staircase when Lee had parties. I scuffled my shoes on the welcome mat, trying to get off as much of the damp as I could, but I still squeaked on the wooden floors.

Music pumped out of speakers, and all of the people I used to know were looking at me like they were playing

"One of these things is not like the other." I made for the kitchen, opened Lee's fridge, and found a beer.

"Hey man, you made it." Josh slapped me on the back. "Let's get shit-housed."

Josh grabbed two six-packs from the fridge and set us up in the living room, on a couch backed by the piano and a ten-foot-high window covered by blinds and curtains. Josh got to work, drinking beer and waiting for business.

"What do you think?" he said. "Good to be back in action?"

"It's good," I said.

"It's awesome. We all missed you. It's always, like, where the hell is Hunter? Is he sitting at home, jerking off in his room? Watching re-runs of *Friday Night Lights* and rubbing one out to Minka Kelly?"

He let out a laugh, a short bark, knowing that people were there to see him and he had the lines to make them hang around, just waiting for him to do something cool.

"If Niall were here, it'd be the whole family," he added.

"You didn't even want him around," I said.

"Yeah, not when he got fucking crazy. But when he was a little bit of crazy, that was pretty cool. It's a fine line, man."

I couldn't remember exactly when Josh stopped wanting to have Niall around. Six months after Niall put that piano bench through the window, I'd invite him over and he'd say, "Is Crazy Niall going to be there?" and I'd have to answer yes. Josh didn't make up excuses. He didn't pretend. "Cool. Have fun, man," he'd say and hang up the phone. The same thing happened with Lee, just a couple of months before Josh stopped thinking Niall was worth it.

A couple of guys hung around with us at first, buying a little weed and smoking up with me and Josh on Lee's couch. It was a weight off my shoulders, a sinking back into the cushions. I was four beers deep, and happy, when people started noticing me there. A couple of them looked at me sideways, peripheral vision sizing me up and figuring out how I'd changed. I wanted to tell them that they couldn't even know. That they didn't want to.

I drank too fast. My six-pack was gone. I told Josh I was going to find a bathroom. I was floating across the carpet, not even feeling the shoulders and knees and elbows digging themselves into my body when I walked through the crowd. A line-up for the bathroom had formed by the kitchen, and the one down the hall by the room that Lee's dad kept as his office. I was out of it enough that I headed up the staircase, the one that should have had the "Forbidden—No Trespassers" sign up but, with the way my eyes were blurring, I wouldn't have seen a thing like that anyway.

I used the bathroom at the top of the stairs. There was another one in the master bedroom and another one attached to Lee's, but I was still sober enough to know that those two were out of bounds. I washed my hands and used the soap pump, this vanilla foam that was the exact same smell as Lee.

She was standing by the bathroom door when I came out. Her dress was short and her legs didn't stop, not even when they hit her feet, a pair of grey socks pulled up at the bottom of her tights.

"What are you doing up here?"

"Bathroom," I said, jerking my thumb at the door. I was losing it, my tenuous hold on normality.

"No one's allowed up here. And I didn't invite you."

"Josh did. He told me to come."

"Yeah, well, I didn't invite him, either."

It wasn't the right time to be noticing Lee, her hair falling out of her ponytail and her earrings getting lost in her hair. It wasn't the right time to lose the lines of communication between my brain and my body. And it definitely wasn't the right time to lean in and try to kiss her with beer breath and drunk lips, but I did it anyway.

She pulled away.

"Hunter, go home."

"I miss you," I said.

"No, you don't. You miss Niall. No one's going to be a stand-in for him. Trust me, no one's even going to try."

My head was swimming. It was a fishbowl, and I swear I could feel something like a pair of fins rubbing against my brain.

I turned back down the stairs. Lee would stay upstairs until she was sure that I was gone, and then she'd go back down and maybe hook up with some guy and talk about it with her friends in the morning.

I missed the last bus home. I had to walk, hunching my shoulders against the cold.

Frost in the morning.

On the Bus

Lee fell asleep somewhere between Banff and Golden. I didn't think about how far she'd had to come in just a few days, and how far we still had to go. This was a round-trip for her with just a day in the middle.

It's selfish to believe that the people you leave behind will stay the same until you come back. But this Lee was the same Lee that I knew from before. She still had shoulder-length hair and it was back in a ponytail. She dressed the same. She still lugged her canvas bag over her left shoulder.

She was still holding my hand when she fell asleep, so I just removed mine and placed hers back on her thigh. Then I went across the aisle and sat with Poppy.

"So," I said, "how's everything?"

"It's fine," she said.

"Yeah? You like traveling by bus?"

She rolled her eyes at me. For just a second, they both went zombie white.

Getting her to talk had always been tooth-pulling difficult but, since we'd got on the bus, it had gotten even harder. I was asking all the wrong questions. I was acting like she was five years old. *Are you hungry? Are you okay? Do you like buses? Goo goo ga.*

I clenched my hands, trying to ask her the thing I'd been worrying about since we left Lethbridge.

"Do you think your mom will have noticed you're gone yet?"

"Probably not," Poppy said, making it casual. "She was going Christmas shopping all morning. What's your aunt going to do when she sees you're gone?"

I shrugged. I hadn't thought a lot about what Aunt Lynne would do. I'd been living at her house in Lethbridge for the last three months. I didn't know how she'd react to me being gone. I'd left her a note. A half-assed explanation. *Going home to Victoria. It's Niall. I'll be back.* I had more grace time than Poppy did because my aunt was going to be out until after dinner.

"I guess she'll call my parents," I said.

"You're lucky she's your aunt and not your mom."

"Nah, I kind of wish she was sometimes. She's pretty good at it."

Even though Poppy played it off, I was still panicked about what her mom would do.

Talking to Poppy, I had double-vision. There were two of her—the Poppy on the bus, and the Poppy who maybe hated me a little because I'd done a stupid thing the day before. I'd snooped around and found something I shouldn't have. I opened a box. The one with her dad's secret folded inside. I wasn't going to forget her face. Surprised, shocked, hurt.

"Pops," I said, "we should talk about what happened."

"I don't want to talk right now," she said.

"I shouldn't have been snooping."

"Hunter," she said. Her pointy knuckles got me in the ribs. I made an *oof*. "We're on a shitty bus. We're on a shitty bus for, like, twenty more hours. Don't be a jerk."

"Okay, okay," I said.

I faced forward. Looked past the old lady with her beady eyes and crow beak, and up to the front of the bus. A hipster couple sat directly behind the bus driver. They were older than me and Lee, but I wouldn't call them grown-ups. They held hands over the armrest. The boy had curly hair and the girl had thick bangs that were saved from falling into her eyes by a pair of big-framed glasses. I could see the screen of their MacBook. Some romance movie they were watching together.

"You've got enough to eat?" I didn't know why I brought up food with Poppy, like I could tell if she was okay based on whether or not she was eating enough of the crap junk food we had brought along. She just nodded.

That was my second worry, after what Poppy's mom was going to do. What if something happened to Poppy while she was with me on this trip? My one decision to take her with us could make everything go wrong. She looked so small and so young in her seat. Those straight-across bangs weren't helping.

"Hey," I said, "you want to play a game?"

"What kind?"

"See who can spot the first bear?"

"They're all hibernating," she said. "It's winter."

"First moose?"

Poppy sighed but looked out the window anyway. All you could see were thick fir trees with their needles pressing into the needles of the tree next door. The way the bus drove along so fast blurred them all together, a mash-up of green that made me kind of vomit-y. The banks of snow were built up high, and we were lucky the weather was holding up on our trip through the mountains. The winter roads that climbed the mountains and then dove back down them again got a little deadly sometimes.

"There," Poppy said. "A moose."

We'd driven past before I could see if it was really there or not.

"Oh, yeah? What'd it look like?"

"Antlers," Poppy said, making pretend ones with her hands and sticking them to the top of her head. "Big ones."

"Cool," I said. "You win."

We both kept staring out the window. I didn't know if we were playing the game anymore. If we were, we were both losing.

As we slowed down on the highway, Poppy said, "I see another one." Something was on the road ahead, and a man in a bright orange and yellow vest held up a stop sign. We were fifth in a line of traffic.

"See one what?" I said.

"Another moose."

Poppy had her finger pointed and pressing against the window.

I couldn't see it right away. I thought she was pulling my leg, count to ten and she'd tell me she was joking. But then a couple of branches stopped being branches and turned into the antlers that they were. I could see the big brown snout, those two black eyes, the ears pointing at the sky. The moose stood stock still, staring at the side of the bus.

"Holy shit. That thing is huge."

"It's a giant," Poppy said, turning to me with this grin.

We watched the moose until the bus started moving again. Then, it blended back into the forest, still standing in the exact same place as it always had been.

No one else on the bus was looking out the window. They were watching movies on laptops, or reading books, or talking on the phone. A couple of people were sleeping. The moose had stepped out of the woods for only me and Poppy to see. Pointing its antlers in the direction of home and sending us on our way.

That morning at school, Lee came around the corner, right toward me. Her hair was down and she wasn't wearing makeup, the only girl at our school who could pull that off. Hot with embarrassment, I ducked into the bathroom, sat in the stall, and pushed my feet up against the door. I couldn't stop thinking about the way Lee had looked at me when I tried to kiss her.

I was looking as rough as I felt. My sneakers were beat up, scuffed, and discolored from rain and walking home. The rubber soles falling off, the bottoms coming undone. Frayed jeans, the legs wet and grungy. Holey sweater and unwashed shirt. Mom and Dad didn't have a clue about what was going on with me. They were at work, Dad sitting at his desk and rolling between computer and phone on his ergonomic black leather chair, Mom standing on a yoga mat, adjusting all the women stretching. They were probably figuring that they had done pretty good, all odds against and stuff. Bridget living on her own with a job, and me finishing up high school soon. They saw my friendship with Niall as a blip on the timeline of my life, something that only needed monitoring infrequently. Normal kids, normal life. It wasn't their fault they didn't see all the shit that went down with Niall, but they weren't looking for it and I wasn't volunteering.

Niall wasn't a blip. He was my best friend. Even when it was up and down, I still knew him better than almost anyone else. But sometimes it was scary how he could get. He would change in the amount of time it took for you to snap your fingers.

The summer before, we had met up at the fair. I found him in the middle of a group of people, laughing so hard his Adam's apple bobbed up and down. When I joined them, he said, "I was looking for you."

"Yeah. Big place."

"Hunter," Josh said. He bobbed his head at me. "How's it going, man?" He slipped something in my hand and, without even looking, I swallowed it down.

"Thanks," I said.

"Thanks and twenty bucks," he corrected.

"No cash," I said, holding up my hands.

"You want to owe me?"

I shrugged a yes.

It was six of us there together and we went on every ride. I threw up three times, once in one of those green garbage cans with the opening just wide enough for an empty pop bottle.

Later we grabbed a couple of burgers and ate them at a wooden picnic table. Niall covered for me, doling out twenties that I promised to pay back. It was dark and the overhead lights had all turned on. The music was louder, pumping out of the speakers in a way that I could really feel.

"What was that stuff?" I asked Josh.

He shrugged his shoulders, cracking a smile.

I think a lot of people at school missed his good moments. Niall's. They didn't see him screaming his head off on the roller coaster, his teeth showing and his hair covering his eyes. They didn't see him lifting the safety bar over his shoulders, looking uncertain, wondering if that bar was really going to keep him from flying.

Later that night, when we were all sitting at a table and I was thinking about heading home, Niall went quiet. I felt it growing, the way he could get in the middle of a crowd of people.

"Hey, Niall, you ready to go?" I asked.

Niall stared up at the Ferris wheel, the ride closest to us. He was already gone, sliding comatose, eyes wide open. It wasn't a lot but it freaked Josh out, the way Niall could just shut down and vacate.

But it didn't come out of nowhere. I'd been over to Niall's house and knew I'd be as wrecked as he was if I had to live there. The big empty space where his sister was supposed to be, and his parents turned into shut-ins. Somehow me and Josh had gotten Niall to check back in again, even if it was a little irregularly, but that didn't mean we could erase everything else that was wrong with his life.

"Dude, why are you doing this?" Josh asked him. "Just be normal. We're having fun."

Niall didn't answer. He just slid his eyes from the Ferris

wheel to Josh, a heavy dragging that almost made me get out of there.

"No, I'm serious," Josh said. "Forget this shit. It's only eleven. I'm going on some rides."

"I think I'm going home," Niall said.

"Come on," Josh said, pulling on the back of Niall's shirt. "Don't be a dick."

It happened so fast—the hard crack, the wet thump, and Niall's fist moving back from Josh's face to his side.

Josh went down hard.

I yelled at Niall, "What'd you do?" But he was already out of there.

I looked at Josh, flat on the ground, a couple of the guys we were with checking to see if he was all right. His eyes twitched open, first one, then the other. I waited to see that he was fine. Then I went after Niall.

When we walked home together, I looked in the window of one of the downtown stores and saw my face looking back. My eyes looked like Niall's, pupils huge and black. When I turned up my street to go home, Niall said, "You're as crazy as me." He said it like a compliment. A good thing.

I was thinking about that day at the fair, when the door to the bathroom at Douglas flapped open and Josh said, "Hunter, dude, I know you're in here."

I dropped my feet from the door, came out of the stall, leaned against the counter, and smoked up with Josh, the two of us getting comfortable before we started talking.

"I was thinking," I told him, "about that night at the fair."

Josh rubbed his chin and let out a bark of a laugh.

"Crazy Niall," he said. "What a dick. Knocked me right out. But he got back what was coming to him." Josh repaid him a couple of nights later and, after that, there was no more Niall and Hunter and Josh. Josh bowed out, just like Lee had. What happened to Niall was just a couple of months later, over Christmas holidays. "He was so much work," Josh said. "Everyone always had to figure out how to act around him, so it didn't set him off."

"Doesn't mean it's okay, what happened to him."

Josh smoked the rest of the joint without offering it back to me. He was about to head back to class when he turned around, remembering that he had a gift for me. I took the pills. Josh gave me an army salute and went back into the hallway. A couple of seconds later, I followed him.

At lunch, I sat at a table with Josh in the cafeteria, eating greasy burgers and soggy fries. It almost felt like old times. It wasn't just me and Josh at the table. It was us and everybody we knew, the table full and cool, with people swiveling their heads to check us out. Josh made sure I was taken care of, leaving me in the conversational hands of Jordan before he hit the vending machine for a Coke.

"Long time, no see," Jordan said. "You doing okay?"

"I'm fine."

"You done hanging out by yourself?"

"Looks like it."

Jordan snorted, kicked back a couple of fries. "Seriously, though, you're back now?"

"Yeah."

"Watch it, hey? You're not the only one messed up by

what happened to Niall."

I had known Jordan since I started high school, a big guy with the football thing going on, freezing his ass off on Friday nights out on the field behind the school. We didn't have much to say, not before and not now. Jordan zipped and unzipped his backpack, checked his phone, and then put an ear bud in his right ear, and, what do you know, I was sitting to the right of him. He waited a couple of minutes before he grabbed his stuff and peaced out of there.

"See you in class, man."

"Later."

Josh nodded at me from across the table, his nod syncopating with the sound of the bell ringing. I left for Chem. There was a single narrow window at the back of the small classroom on the second floor, a whiteboard, projector, desks, and tables filling up the rest. Chem was quizzes and tests, questions and answers. It was sitting at the back of the room being bored, watching the clock, and listening to its painfully slow tick-tock.

"Settle down. Get out your books and let's start."

Ms. Reed had her go-to sentences for starting the class, and that was the nicest.

"Hunter," Ms. Reed said. "Nice to have you with us."

So maybe I had been skipping a bit. Leaving school after lunchtime. Nice of her to notice.

"Thanks."

"We'll talk after class. Okay, everyone, page one hundred and fifty-five in your textbook. Let's go."

Ms. Reed turned her back to us about a quarter of the

way through class to write on the board. She drew a flow diagram and boxed off the labels that explained how all of the parts worked together. Everyone copied it down. When Reed made a mistake, her easy swipe of the eraser across the white board was a whole lot neater than my scratched-out pen and mess of a page. After that, Reed divided us into groups to do a worksheet, a "find the answer in the text book." She numbered us off—one, two, three, four—and sent us to different zones. Two lucky groups hit pay dirt and got sent to the library, where the librarian stayed in his office and didn't check on noise or production levels.

My group was Mark and Travis and Sarah. We sat at a table, two across from two, books open to different pages. They talked and flipped through, looking for answers, reluctantly bringing me into the fold.

"So, you're sticking around all day now," Travis said. He had been sitting at the other end of the table at lunch, and I figured he had been keeping an eye out. "You back or something?"

"I guess."

There wasn't much eye contact. What did I have except empty spaces and empty places?

"I don't even know how to pronounce this word," Sarah said, pointing at mitochondria. It was in her Bio textbook, and she was working on the homework for Kesler's class from that morning. We followed her lead and dragged out our papers and textbook from the morning's Bio class, and covered them with our Chem textbooks, the spines pointing out.

"Mi-to-chon-dri-a," Mark said, pronouncing each of its five syllables.

"It's not in the back of the book," Sarah said.

Travis found it a few minutes later and we tried re-working the definition, changing the order of "a" and "the" to make it look different, not word-for-word.

"I can't find the answer to number six," Sarah said, and none of us could either. She sighed and went over to another group to outsource the answer.

"So, you have to see Penner," Travis said to me when she was gone.

"Yep. Friday Psych Day."

"You're seeing him because of what happened to Niall?"

Label the parts of a typical animal cell and show their subcellular components. Mark was looking at me. Both of them waiting for an answer.

"No," I said.

Mark flipped through the pages of his textbook, pretending not to listen. His eyes locked on mine for a few seconds, a "Careful, man, you messed up, getting Travis on your back."

"It doesn't make sense that you're still here," he said. "And he isn't."

Travis had a fist formed nice and neat and, coincidence, I had one, too.

"It's not like you were the only person who hung around with him," he said. "But you're the one who fucked everything up."

I punched Travis across the desk just before he got me.

Left eye, black, blank, starry. Mark grabbed his other arm to pull him back, but that fist came again and knocked me in the jaw. This crack and my teeth grinding together, one a little loose and sore. My hands were balled up and I was ready to give him something back. Instead, I sank, an overwhelming weight letting go, and let him hit me.

Reed called across the hall and a couple of teachers came in and got Travis off of me. Reed grabbed my arms and the classroom went unfamiliar.

"Hunter," Reed said. "You need to go to the office."

"Yeah, sure," I said. My mouth wasn't making words the way it usually did. Each one was heavy and weighted.

"Right away," she said. "I'm phoning ahead."

The first place I went was the bathroom. Broken doors and cracked floor. Smell of weed in the air because me and Josh didn't hide shit. My name was going all over the intercom. "Hunter Ryan to the office, please. Hunter Ryan." It followed me all the way out of the school and into the woods and back to that wall, the one that me and Niall found, the place that felt like flying.

I was in my bedroom on Mom's laptop, refreshing Facebook, checking out what everybody else was up to—party pictures, updates, and check-ins downtown—and feeling that pit in my chest. It was depressing as hell when I had nothing going on.

The whole day had been like that. I took a nap in my bed, curtains open, sun in, and ate a bag of chips in front of the computer. My black eye, courtesy of Travis, was looking bad and there was no way I was going to school. Instead I checked out Lee's Facebook profile and looked at old photos from the year before.

The thing about Lee was that I'd known her for forever. Mom said we went to kindergarten together. That was our start point, back when we were five years old. If we had a start point, then we had an end point. Jason Guerra's party at the end of last summer, just before school started.

A bunch of us went up to his attic, locking ourselves in by accident, after closing up the trap door with its slanted stairs behind us. Lee brought up a bottle of vodka and Josh kept the joints going around in a circle. I was getting shittier and shittier up in that attic. Music was playing on the first floor, but we only got the tail end of it all the way upstairs, the ba-boom ba-boom ba-boom of bass. Locked in and messed up enough that we didn't care how long we were stuck up there for. Josh pissed out the window and Lee's friend did it, too, hanging out ass backwards and laughing her head off.

Lee was sitting beside me, our knees knocking and her hand on my thigh, closer and closer to where I wanted it to be. Across from me was Niall, getting quiet, and I should've known what was coming and got him out of there. Signs and crossings. Hints and dead giveaway.

"Dude, tell us about that time you wanted to time travel your dead cat," Josh said, killing himself laughing. He was talking to Niall, wanting him to look like a freak in front of everybody else sitting in the attic.

"Come on," Lee whispered to me. "Like we haven't heard this before."

She grabbed my hand, knit her fingers between mine, and took me over to the far side of the attic, where castaway furniture was stacked seat-to-seat. She grabbed me so my back was making waves with a ratty old couch, turned vertical for storage.

"God, I'm drunk," Lee said, turning a circle on her toes, my hand holding hers above her head.

"Me, too."

"How much weed does Josh give you?"

"A lot," I said, thinking about the whiff I got walking by my closet, even though it was hidden, Russian-doll style, inside a bag inside an envelope inside a shoebox under a pile of clothes.

"Your brain's fucked," she said.

"My brain's relaxed as hell. It's taking off."

Lee laughed and lined up our hips, hipbone to hipbone, pressing my back firmly against the couch. Pieces of Niall were escaping from the circle, and I was trying to ignore them.

Lee stepped her feet in between mine and we were closer than close. Her hands slid into the loops of my belt, one dipping into my back pocket, the other inching up the bottom of my shirt.

We'd never fooled around like that before, me and Lee, until there was that couch acting like the third person that held me up against her. We made out at the back of the attic, everybody else only a couple of feet away, talking normally and knowing just exactly what we were doing. We pushed down the couch, vertical to horizontal, grungy cushions and dust. Lee was on her back making me the visible one, and I didn't even give a shit.

"Hey," she said. "I wanted it to be me and you."

"Me, too."

She made a face, knew I was an idiot even behind the smokescreen of drunk. She made out with me anyway, unhooking her bra when my hands stopped working, clumsy and fat-fingered. She laughed into my cheek, going in for a kiss but finding something funny instead. I had my lips on her eyebrow, the most hilarious thing, and I put my tongue under the arch and kissed her there, too.

Niall picked that moment exactly to start swearing at some guy over on the other side of our furniture fort. I opened my eyes, heavy and thick-lidded. Lee kept kissing me, my eyes wide open.

I leaned over the armrest to see who Niall had picked to lose it with. I still don't know who he was. Just a guy.

"Hunter!" Josh yelled. "Niall's going crazy."

Lee's hand slid into my pocket, her fingers pinching my ass. A do-not-move, Hunter Ryan, stay here.

"He's killing this kid!"

Niall had the guy on the ground, his fist moving in a mechanical up-and-down into his face. I vaulted off the couch and helped Josh pull Niall off him. Someone had the window open and the attic was clearing out, everyone sliding down the roof to get to the ground below.

After, when Niall was calmer, Josh gave me a salute and headed to the window. Niall wasn't his problem. He was just along for the ride.

"What happened?" I asked him.

Josh looked at Niall. "Doesn't matter how messed up you are, it doesn't mean you can do shit like this."

He slid out the window.

That left Lee—fixing her clothes and leaning against the window—Niall, and me.

"You coming, Hunter?"

I looked between her and Niall. I shook my head. "I can't."

Lee kicked the couch at me and slid out the window. No goodbye.

Me and Niall sat on the floor and smoked a joint.

"What happened?" I asked him.

"I don't know."

"He say something to you?"

Niall shrugged. "I guess not," he said. "I don't know."

"Is this because of what happened to your sister?"

He didn't give me an answer. Whatever made Niall the way he was, he wasn't talking about it.

When the music stopped on the floor below, we went out the window, split at the end of the street and went our separate ways home.

I was thinking about that party when Lee called. I pressed the phone against my ear, feeling the crick work its way into my neck, dig deep, and sit there. I was using the portable from downstairs, my cell phone buried at the bottom of my backpack. I clicked out of Facebook and swiveled away from the computer.

"Josh says you're back," Lee said.

"I guess."

"Well, what is it? Back or still being an asshole?"

"Back," I said. "Back."

I let the silence climb to reach her end and mine, pooling in the wires and getting our signals crossed. Me and Lee were just radio frequencies finally tuned to the right channel.

"Lee?" I asked. "Why are you calling?"

Lee sighed on the other end of the phone. "I don't know, okay? I've been thinking a lot."

"Do you want to get coffee or something?" I asked her, fumbling. "We could talk."

"No," she said. "I mean, not tonight. This is enough, you know?"

I was trying to fill the gap between us. When it became too much work, I left it and let it fall. It was my fault we were even there at all. Made my bed, had to lie in it.

"I have to go," Lee said. "I just wanted to call. You doing okay? Heard you got into a fight."

"I'm fine," I said.

"Good," she said. "That's good."

She hung up the phone after that and I was alone in my room again. Except this time I had Lee in my head, Lee in miniature banging on the inside of my brain.

I went to the mirror and checked out my eye. Black and purple and an ugly yellow around the center. Then I fell back on my bed and stared at the ceiling, wishing I could program sleep until Niall woke up.

On the Bus

"Hey." Lee nudged my shoulder with her chin, just waking up. "Where are we?"

"We're in Golden in a sec," I told her. "We can get off for a couple of minutes, even. Hour nine out of twenty-seven, Lee. We're getting there."

"'Kay," she said. "Maybe I'll call my dad."

"Hey," I said, touching her shoulder. "It's golden Golden."

The bus came to a stop.

"Pops, you want to come?" I asked her, standing up and reaching my arms right up over my head.

"Nah," she said. "I'm good."

"Any requests?" Lee asked her.

Poppy sat carefully, holding her back straight so that it just barely touched the back of the seat. Before she'd been as slouched as a laundry bag full of clothes. She was suddenly princess-in-training, practicing her etiquette and posture. She shook her head. "No, I don't want anything."

I didn't want to leave Poppy there, but Lee was already grabbing my hand and pulling, and then we were out the double doors and in the cool, dim air.

I waved at Poppy from outside. She didn't wave back.

"Come on," Lee said. "I want a second, just you and me."

"That's new," I said. Lee pinched my wrist, but nicely. My skin went pink and then white again.

She pulled me into a bookstore across the street from where the bus was parked. She wiped her boots furiously on the carpet by the door. Snow was on the ground and had been since Calgary. It was a genuine Winter Wonderland. There was a foot of it here in Golden, fresh and powdery, and you could tell tomorrow was going to be a good day on the mountain. I took a couple of looks over my shoulder at the bus, trying to find Poppy's face at the window.

"Hunter," Lee said, pulling me to the back of the store, "I need to find something to read for the rest of the way."

"Why don't you get a magazine?" I was thinking about those *Us Weekly* magazines Aunt Lynne was always reading. There was some good stuff in there. Celebrities without makeup was my favorite. A lot of those actresses looked rough.

"I read those on the way here. I'm gossiped out."

The store was busy but, at the back, it was just us. Lee thumbed through the fiction section, working her way alphabetically down the shelf.

"Are you going to tell me what's up with Poppy now?" she asked me.

"Nothing's up with her. She's just along for the ride."

"You *said* you'd explain." Lee pulled a book off the shelf.

How to explain Poppy. I cleared my throat awkwardly. Coughed up a hairball. Frog in my throat.

"She's twelve," I said. I hoped that would cover it.

It didn't.

"Exactly," Lee said. "Twelve-year-olds can stay home by themselves. It's not like you had to drag her along with us. It's weird."

"I couldn't just leave her there," I told her, not explaining anything. "You can't just leave a kid in a big empty house."

"You can if it means not kidnapping her." Lee lowered her voice on the word "kidnapping."

"You know we're not doing that."

"Even if you don't call it that, it's basically the same thing," Lee said. "Her mom doesn't even know she's gone. You ever heard of an 'Amber Alert,' Hunter? Those things are serious."

"It's nothing like that," I said. "I know her. And leaving her alone without an explanation would have been worse than taking her with us. So what if we have to explain to her mom, eventually? You have to know that's better than us leaving her alone."

Plus I messed it all up, I thought. Leaving after finding that box, Poppy's sad-fish face the last thing I'd seen, wasn't even a possibility. I couldn't leave it like that.

Lee snuck a peek out the window at the bus.

"How do you even know a twelve-year-old kid well enough to be worried about her?"

"We're homeschooled together," I told her. "The whole time I've been in Lethbridge, three whole months."

"That still doesn't explain why she's here," Lee said, crossing her arms in front of her chest.

"I know," I said. "I can't really. She's going through some stuff, I think." *And I want her here*, I thought. *I didn't want to do this on my own.*

"You think her mom will send the police? When she sees she's gone?"

"No," I said. "No."

But I didn't know. Give or take an hour, which was when Poppy's mom would get home to that empty house. I didn't know what she was going to do when she found it *sans* Poppy. How long would it take for her to guess that Poppy was with me, just like she was every day? How long would it take to call the Greyhound? How long would it take for them to catch up to us? It was my fault she was here, instead of at home where she should be. It was selfish all the way through. She was here because I wanted her to be.

The cover of the book Lee held under her arm was dark navy blue with geometric shapes intersecting in the middle. It looked like something that would be in class sets at Douglas High. Read chapter by chapter over the course of the entire year. It took a billion years to read a fiction book in English class.

"We better go," she said.

Then she did something that hadn't happened for more than a year. She leaned right in and touched her lips on mine and held them there. As quick as she did it, she moved away, heading to the register to buy her book. Almost like it was unreal, I put my hand to my mouth, feeling the warmth.

A couple of days after I talked to Lee on the phone, I left for school an hour early. The damp climbed down into my chest and took a seat. The fog was burning off the ocean but, twenty minutes earlier, it would've been a wall of blindness shielding the island. I got on a bus and took it into Oak Bay, watched the wave of big house, big house, mansion, big house, mansion, mansion. Lee's house was out of the way, the opposite direction from Douglas. She would get into her car every morning and gun it so she would get there just a couple of seconds before the bell rang. I knocked on Lee's door and waited on the front steps.

I had only seen her once that whole week. Wednesday in the hallway. I was standing at my locker, spinning the dial, and there was the back of her head, walking away from me. No Lee at lunch, not sitting on the other side of Josh at the cafeteria table. No waving at her in the parking lot after school, hoping for a ride home. She called to check on me once and then it was like she realized she'd overstepped. Time to back off again.

Opening the door, Lee's mother said, "Hunter. We haven't seen you for a while." She traveled all over the place with her husband, so it made sense that she didn't know shit about the parties that went on when they were gone.

"Yeah, well, it's been busy."

"Are you here for Lee?"

"Is she still around?"

Mrs. McKenzie retreated into her house, leaving me in the entranceway, the door still cracked an inch. The straps of my backpack were hanging one over each shoulder. I let one go, shouldering it all on the left.

"What are you doing here?" Lee had her feet planted hip-width, one hand rumpling the bottom of her sweater.

"Morning," I said.

"Hunter, I didn't say you could do this. We didn't talk about you coming over here."

"I know. I thought maybe we could drive to school together or something. Talk in the car."

"Not a good idea."

"It's what, five, ten minutes to get there?"

"You should've called."

"If I called first, you would've told me not to come over. Come on. Five minutes."

Lee looked behind her into the house. Without saying a word, she walked back down the hall. The faint clink of dishes hitting together barely made it all the way to the front to reach me.

I felt like an asshole, throwing the other strap of my backpack over my shoulder again, working out the bus schedule in my head to figure out if I'd miss first period. I closed the heavy door behind me, erasing the inch Lee left behind, and headed down the driveway.

"What the hell, Hunter?" Lee said, popping her head out the door. "Just give me a sec."

She followed down the front steps after me, heading for her car. She stuck the key in the driver's side and mechanically opened the passenger door. I climbed in, stuffed my backpack by my feet, and seat-belted myself in.

Some song came on the radio, loud and blaring, the noise left over from the last time she drove. Lee casually turned it down again, high, middle, low.

"What do you want to talk about?" she asked, abrupt.

"Are we cool?"

"No."

"I mean, can we go back to normal?"

"No."

"Why?"

Lee made the turns, right, left, right, through the residential and out onto the main road. The traffic was backed up, the right and left lanes taking turns going around the cherry picker parked on the side of the street. There was a man up there with a chainsaw, taking down branches from an old tree, the ones that crossed over the entire road.

"Different people, Hunter," she said. "You changed a lot hanging out with Niall all the time, and I did, too."

"I kind of changed back."

"No, you didn't," she said. "And if you did, you're an idiot. No one goes back."

It was our turn to swerve around the cherry picker, the woman in the orange vest turning her STOP sign into a SLOW sign. Lee didn't go slow. She whipped around the blockage, swerving wildly.

After that it was a couple more turns and we were at the school parking lot. There wasn't much left in the way of empty spots. The bell was about to ring and everyone was already parked, walking from their cars to the school. Lee found a space at the back of the lot, squeezed between two asshole parkers who had their tires on the yellow lines. I opened my door hard into the truck next to us and left a good-sized dent.

"I thought we were good," I said.

Lee walked ahead of me into the school.

"So you're back," Lee said. "But maybe we finally got used to you being gone."

I went through the motions of my classes. A little Bio, some Math, some Chem, and Spanish. Each one sucked harder than the one that came before it, teachers getting more worn out after lunch. The ones in the morning were bitching about how early it was and making excuses to hit up the teacher's lounge to get another cup of coffee. I kept my head down and didn't talk to anyone. Josh tried to get me out of it at lunch, driving us off campus and hot-boxing his car down a residential street. I told him about going to Lee's first thing, and he barked out his dog laugh and slapped me on the back. I was the only one who forgot how to play it cool.

At the end of the day, I watched Lee start the drive

home, hers the first car out of the parking lot.

So I ended up stuffing my books and backpack into the bottom of my locker and catching a bus downtown. The buses after school were packed full, standing-room only. There was no bar left to hold onto, only the canvas straps hanging from the ceiling. It was worse than an amusement park ride, stomach going up and then down again a thousand times over until the bus stopped. People pushed past me, and I sandwiched myself between bodies and walls and windows to let them by. The bus driver stopped letting people on when we were halfway to downtown, and we sped up then. I took an empty seat.

I got off by the big Chapters and then walked down the street to the bookstore Bridge worked at. She was standing behind the counter, scanning a few books and bagging them, slipping in a couple of bookmarks for free. She had been working double time that week, not showing her face around the house. I had this idea in my head about checking in on her, but there was nothing she needed me for.

I unlocked Bridget's apartment with the key from Mom's keychain and I was in before anyone saw me. The apartment was bare. The cupboards were empty. The living room echoed. Bridge's bathroom had the basics— toothbrush, toothpaste, brush, hair dryer—neatly in order. There was a bed in her room, but the closets were empty. An open suitcase was on the floor, the few obvious pieces of clothing folded inside. I climbed up on her bed and sat on the sheets. The pictures that Mom had forced me to hang up were gone, just the indent of nails still visible in the wall.

The dresser we lugged up the flight of stairs was gone. So were the bookshelf and all the books that had been on it. So much for moving her in just a year ago.

My wallet sat in my back pocket, reminding me about Josh and the gifts he'd been giving me over the last few weeks. Him holding out his Altoids and giving me my pick. I never took them, not after Josh's trick with the Tylenol. Now I had a good collection, all of those pills lined up on the sheets, white on blue. I went down the row, methodically swallowing one pill after the other.

I started with one pill and then nothing stopped me from taking another. And another. The empty apartment, the fight at school, how cold Lee was. There wasn't a good thing to hold on to. There wasn't anything to pull me up and out of the water and drag me back into the real world.

Niall was right about checking out. It was the easiest thing.

I had a seriously heavy head by the time I had taken all of the pills. They pushed me back and I made nice with the pillow, comfy as anything behind my head. I didn't have working hands to put my wallet back in my pocket, so it sat out on the bed and smiled at me lazily, the two of us waiting for everything to kick in.

I stared at the ceiling in Bridget's bedroom for what might have been a half-hour. Pills working their magic on my system.

I thought about it all the time.

Just a couple of days before Christmas, I had left the house first thing in the morning. I didn't take anything with me, just got my bike out of the garage and went over to Niall's. He was out front, standing at the sidewalk, looking like some kid who was waiting for his parents to pick him up from school. I stashed my bike in his garage. It's still there.

Niall lived in the perfect neighborhood, walking distance everywhere. It was a fifteen-minute walk to the beach. We didn't talk on the way there. Maybe three cars drove by. The sun was barely up but it was going to be shining. December in Victoria. Sitting in boats out on the ocean if you dressed warm enough.

When the road turned into the marina, Niall led the way to his family's boat. I followed behind him, no clue where he was taking us.

"You okay?" Niall asked.

"I'm fine."

The beach was right in front of us, sandy, rocks and driftwood. The water was still.

We lowered the boat into the ocean, fast and smooth, and sat down inside. The motor was a low hum. There wasn't a reason to talk.

I didn't go out on the ocean that much. I'd taken the ferry over to Vancouver a couple of times with Mom and Dad, when we'd family vacation over to the lakey interior. A couple of my friends had kayaks but they paddled close to the shore. Every minute that passed on the ocean with Niall was further out than I'd ever been before.

He took us out half an hour before he told me to turn off the motor.

It was so quiet out there. The waves were small and almost

still. It felt like we were in the middle of the ocean.

The sun was up but my hands were freezing. I cupped them together and blew hot air into the gap. Niall did the same. He had on this straight-laced expressed, tied up tight. We didn't touch the stuff Josh had given us. Instead, we sat drifting in that boat, keeping an eye on the right direction back. The sun made us squint at one another, shooting the shit about nothing at all, end-of-school release gone from my chest.

So when he did it, I wasn't even paying attention. I had my arms out behind me, supporting the rest of my body with bent-back wrists.

Niall shoved all of our pills into his mouth and swallowed them down with water.

"Shit," I said. "That's a lot."

He didn't say a word. He brought out a tiny plastic bag from his pocket with at least ten more pills in it. I reached for the bag but I wasn't fast enough. He put the pills in his mouth and gulped them down.

"We should get back," I told him. "Those are going to kick in and wipe you out, man. You might need to go to the hospital."

"Hunter," Niall said, giving me a lazy smile. "I'm fine."

"I don't think so."

"Trust me," he said.

Niall stood up and stepped off the edge of the boat. He hardly made a splash. Just one second he was there and the next he was gone.

"Niall," I said, and then louder, "Niall!"

He didn't come up.

I stood up and the boat jerked in its seasick way. I looked into the water but I couldn't see anything but ripples expanding outward.

I went in after him.

The water was so cold and icy. I dropped down, forgetting to take a breath with me. When I opened my eyes under the water, it was green and murky and dark, and then the navy blue color of nighttime sky, all right under the surface.

I bobbed out of the water for a breath of air. Then I dove down. I threw my arms around, hoping I'd touch him, grab the back of his shirt, drag him up to the surface. I stayed down until my lungs were bursting. I swam down further, panic squeezing at my chest. Niall wasn't anywhere.

When I came to the surface, the boat was far away. I swam back to it and tried again, down into the blue murky water, the salt in my eyes. I stayed down longer than I should have. I could feel it hurting me bad under there.

The boat was even further away the second time. Niall had to be close to it. He wouldn't have drifted this far away. I swam back and I dove again.

I did it three more times. Four. Five.

My lungs were trapped in my chest, useless and empty, when I found him. I got a hand around the hood of his jacket. Bringing him out was quicksand slow. My eyes blurred and refocused, the sun waving at us both from above.

I broke the surface, flipped onto my back, and kicked backwards toward the boat, holding Niall under his armpits.

His face kept sliding under the water. I tried to keep him up and he kept sliding down.

In water, everything is supposed to feel weightless. Hair, arms, legs, they're supposed to float to the surface. Niall wasn't floating to the surface.

I finally heaved Niall into the boat, his head and shoulders followed by his legs. There was almost nothing left for me to get myself in, and then to start the motor and try to remember the direction we were going. My eyes were blurry with salt water and my mouth was so dry.

Niall still wasn't conscious when he finally arrived at the hospital in the back of an ambulance.

"Hunter? Hunter? Hey, are you okay? Hunter?"

I heard Bridget's voice and remembered I was in her apartment. I felt something soft underneath me. Behind my eyes, the VHS kept playing. Niall's smile. The boat tipping. The green water. The absence of light.

Niall's body in the boat ...

Then ... white walls, narrow bed, IV needle in my arm. I needed about three seconds to figure out where I was, and then feel my body parts to remember why I was there.

It came back in pieces when I saw Bridget sitting on a hard-backed plastic chair, her neck cricked to the side, out like a light. I pushed back against the pillows and, inch by inch, I got back into a seated position.

I took inventory. There was my white wristband. Ryan, Hunter. DOB. Telephone number. Health insurance. No date of entry. No idea how long I'd been in or how much longer I'd have to stay.

Either I had been in the hospital overnight and Mom and Dad just went home to catch up on some sleep, leaving Bridget covering, or else this had just happened and they hadn't shown up yet. It was gray and overcast out the window, no way to tell what time of day it was.

"You over trying to kill yourself?"

Bridget scooted her chair forward so she was next to the bed, the legs scraping the floor.

"Took the red pill," I said. "There's no going back from that one."

I made a joke of it. Really, in the pit of my stomach, I wondered: Is that what I meant to do? Was I actually trying? I didn't know.

Bridget punched me in the arm, the one opposite where my IV was running. It was hard enough to hurt, to throw me back against the pillow.

"Don't joke."

"I'm not."

"Do you remember what happened?" Bridget asked. "Because I'll tell you what I know, since I am now an expert in finding someone unconscious for unknown reasons, until the doctors at the hospital say 'overdose' and start talking about pumping your stomach."

All of Josh's gifted pills in a line on Bridget's bed sheets, taken from that Altoids container like mints. Any flavor. Choose your own adventure.

"Shit, Bridge."

"Starting to come back to you? Because there's still a few things we're kind of confused about." She talked, staccato and angry, words, packaged accusations slowly unraveling. What next. What next?

The doctor, my doctor, came in and interrupted. Checked on my veins. Was the IV still in there doing its thing; how was my blood pressure/pulse/heart rate holding up; was I nauseous or sick or messed up? He wasn't asking about the where who what when or why. Doctors specialize and this one wasn't there to talk about my mental health.

Bridget didn't take her eyes off me. When the doctor left again, she jumped right back into her interrogation—bad cop, angry cop, ugly cop—extracting answers.

"Where's Mom and Dad?" I asked her. She looked like she was going punch me again, or else start crying and leave the room.

"You're lucky they aren't here. They're meeting with your psychologist. Way to tell us about that."

"Penner," I supplied.

"They'll be back soon. They didn't even want to leave."

"I bet."

"Stop joking about this. Do you know how stupid you are? Giving up everything in three seconds, or however long it took for you to shove enough pills down your throat to almost kill yourself. It's not a joke. It's not funny, ha-ha, that's a good one. Don't you get that?"

"Look, I didn't try to do anything. I didn't know what I was taking. I took too much, I guess, but I wasn't trying to kill myself, Bridge."

"Why were you at my apartment?"

"No clue, dude. Don't read into it."

Bridget did something funny then. She picked up my hand, the one with the IV, and she held it tight. Her thumb went back and forth over the skin puckered by the needle. Her nail polish was chipped. She asked me if I wanted some water and brought me a plastic cup.

"You're coming home when Mom and Dad get here."

"Great," I said.

"Yeah."

She looked out of place in my hospital room. She was wearing the brightest sweater that day, light red.

"Bridge," I said. "What happened to your place? Where's all your stuff?"

Her hands went back to the bed sheets again. She had a nervous tic that made her look like a crazy person, the one who should be in this bed, obsessing over life and death and dying.

Bridge looked up at me. She had this half-smile on her face.

"Dude," she said, "don't, like, read into it."

Quick as that, she was the normal one, giving me a little glass of water, turning on the hospital TV, and making the bed sheets straight again.

Then she said, "You don't tell Mom and Dad this, I mean, especially while you're in here."

"Yeah, okay."

She tapped her feet on the floor. "I applied for a work visa a couple of months ago. Stuff's not really changing for me here. I'm working at the bookstore; I'm going home; I'm sitting all alone in my apartment; or I'm spending all of my time at Mom and Dad's. And it's not going to change. I'm kind of realizing that."

"Work visa where?"

"Australia." She smiled. "Accents."

"Yeah?"

"Look, I started selling stuff online a while ago, so if I decided not to go, I wouldn't just lose everything. I went piece by piece."

"There's nothing left, Bridge."

"Yeah, well, I'm thinking it's just about time."

"Oh."

"So, you can't keep doing this, okay? Mom and Dad? They don't take this stuff so well."

"And you do?"

She shrugged. "Better than them. Just wait."

Bridget leaned back in her chair. She put her feet up on my hospital bed and pushed at mine where they were hanging out under the sheets. My mouth was dry, but I couldn't remember if I'd smoked a joint at Bridget's. She probably would've said something if the smell was there when she found me. Must have been the tube stuck down my throat, bringing those pills back up.

"Can I have a glass of water?"

Bridget passed the glass across the bed. I took a long drink, estimating the chances that I'd do it again.

Half an hour later, Bridget went downstairs to wait for Mom and Dad and give me some privacy. After a few minutes on my own, Josh came in, my second visitor of the day.

Josh jammed his ugly yellow Nikes into the metal bed frame. My hospital bed. Closed my eyes for a second and I almost forgot I'd tried to kill myself.

"Dude, you out of the woods?" he asked. He was on the back legs of his chair, the front legs rearing.

I was in my open-backed hospital gown, bare ass against the bed sheets. The IV pulled on my wrist when I gave Josh a thumbs-up.

"Sick of the world?" he asked.

"Who isn't?"

He leaned forward. Hospitals did things to your hands. They got restless. Josh was too messed up to realize that he should have been hanging onto the chair or sticking his hands in his pockets. Instead he rolled a joint.

"You took all that shit I gave you?"

"You bet."

He stuffed his bag of weed back into his pocket. He made a halo of smell hang around the bed. The joint was rolled fat and tight.

"I'm going outside to smoke this," he said. "You tagging along?"

I had seen what happened next in movies. Some cancer patient hobbling down the hallway with the back of his gown just barely hanging on by its loosely tied bow. I checked out my IV. It was connected to a metal stand with wheels. I was mobile.

"Check if there's a wheelchair."

Josh tossed me his sweater and went out with his T-shirt on. He came back with a wheelchair and I dropped in. My stomach reminded me what I'd done to it and stirred up the emptiness. The whole room tilted to the side, my eyes went blurry, and the space in front of them turned white. Etch-a-sketch, shaking back out again.

I stuck out an arm to make sure the metal stand and my bag of clear liquid came with me, walking the dog. Josh pushed me down the hall. The open doors to the rooms were windows into some depressing-looking lives. I didn't look long.

"Who told you I was in here?" I asked him. He wheeled me outside, aiming for the opposite exit that my parents would be coming in. Bridget would be on the other side of the hospital, where the parking lot was. It was cool but the sun was out, warming us up from the outside in.

"Someone saw the ambulance outside your sister's place. You were strapped down to one of those boards. EMS workers giving you mouth-to-mouth." We stopped beside a low wall and Josh slid on top of it. I heard the click of his lighter. A couple of seconds and he passed the joint. I breathed in deeper than air and waited for lift-off.

"You going to try to off yourself again?" Josh asked.

"I don't know," I said. "It gets to me all the time. That stuff with Niall."

"Yeah, well. Me, too."

He took back the joint and I didn't see it again.

We were the only two people at that end of the hospital. Most smokers hung out in the courtyard on the other side of the cafeteria windows. It made them look like animals at the zoo, contained behind glass.

Turns out I lost eight hours in total. Passed out at Bridget's, ambulanced over to the hospital, stomach pumped. I wished it was more. One of those stories about some kid sleeping for a hundred years and waking up to find everyone they knew dead and gone. I wanted something different than the same watery sun that was there the day before.

"He's still here," I said.

Josh inhaled. "Niall?"

"Yeah."

"He's a floor above you, man."

Niall had been comatose since that day in the ocean. And me not even visiting him once.

"He looks bad?"

"Not pretty."

Josh jumped off the wall. He rolled the metal stand with the IV bag close enough for me to hold it in my hand again. He started rolling me forward.

"What are you doing?"

"We're going to see him."

I panicked a little, back in my throat, trying to get my words out.

"My parents are going to be here soon to get me."

"Five minutes isn't going to matter."

"Josh."

"He was my friend, too," Josh said.

The wheels rolled smoothly over the linoleum in the atrium. Josh darted for the elevator and we went up to Niall's floor. I felt some serious opposite forces. Elevator going up, body sinking down.

Josh never asked what had happened to Niall. He read it in the newspaper or heard it at the assembly, or got the phone call from my parents. He never came to me and asked what really happened, as if my story and the official story would be different. They weren't. But a lot of people didn't think it was possible for someone just to jump off a boat and then be almost saved from drowning by some kid without a scratch on him. They figured that there had to be more to the story than that.

Josh wheeled me to an open doorway. The blinds were pulled up and the sun was spread across the bed sheets. The machines. They sat around the bed in a circle, blinking and beeping.

Niall had a private room. No skinny curtain divided the room in half, him on one side, another patient on the other. There were no obstacles or barriers to Josh and me walking right in and sitting down.

But I couldn't make myself go any further.

Niall had shrunk so much. His face was pulled tight. His arms were toothpick thin, his knees unbelievably huge. One thick tube stuck out of his mouth, his lips cracked and damaged. The IV was in his arm. His feet were pointing in different directions.

When you know someone so well that you've seen them every day, and you've hung out with them at their house or at your house, and you've passed them in the halls at school, it's so much harder to look at them lying unconscious in a hospital bed.

Josh jerked my wheelchair forward. I threw out my arm,

stopping him from moving me.

"No," I said. "This is good."

"You should talk to him, man," Josh said. "You should say something."

"No," I said.

We stood at the door for a few minutes. It felt eternity-sized. Niall had been lying there for almost six months, Christmas to June. In all that time, he hadn't made a single movement on his own.

I said, "Let's go back."

Josh turned my wheelchair around and pushed me into the hallway and back into the elevator.

"Is he doing any better?" I asked when we were back on my floor.

"Did he look better?"

"Six months is a long time to be hooked up like that."

Josh shrugged and helped me into my bed.

"See you when you're back," he said, leaving.

I sat stiff as a board until my parents came. Once you see someone you know like that, half-size, you can't see them in their original packaging again. You take that step forward and lose the way back.

On the Bus

We got back on the bus. Lee went to sit beside Poppy, leaving me with two seats to myself. I stretched out my legs, putting them at a diagonal.

Movies and TV shows always skipped past the on-the-road part of the story. No one cared about the guy sitting in the backseat of the car, twiddling his thumbs until he got to his destination. No one cared about the person on the bus, head against the window, trying to fall asleep without getting a cricked neck. It was all in-between time.

I wanted to sleep until we got to Victoria. Lee was making me think too much about why she was here, and what changed and how it changed, and when. The graph of our relationship or friendship or knowing each other was this embarrassing wavy line that dipped too close to the x-axis more than once. But she took this bus all the way to find me, to tell me the thing that everybody else was keeping a secret. When I counted that, we were back to somewhere close again.

Lee was digging around in her purse. Who knew what was in there? She used to always have her arm in there up to her elbow, moving things around until she found what she was looking for.

"Hey, I thought you were going to read your new book," I joked.

"I'm getting to it," she said.

They were an odd pair, Poppy and Lee. Lee was taking these teeny, tiny glances at Poppy, her forehead creased in the space between her eyebrows.

Poppy was totally getting in the way of me and Lee sharing some tender moments on the bus. Falling asleep on each other's shoulders. Making out a bit at the back of the bus. It wasn't going to happen.

"You got that much stuff in your purse, Pops?" I asked her. "Lee's is like the bottomless pit. Stick your hand in there and it won't come out again."

"Oh, ha ha," Lee deadpanned. With her hand in her purse, she made her entire arm shake, pretending it was being shredded.

It was lame, but I still let out a horse-snort. Poppy rolled her eyes.

"So let's see yours, Poppy," Lee said.

"My what?"

"Your purse."

"I don't have one. I just throw my stuff in a backpack."

"Oh," Lee said. Girly stuff was kind of her selling point. She used to get judgmental about shit like this, girls not being feminine enough. The fact that Poppy was younger made it hard for her to be too mean. Lee's face was complicated. Somewhere in there, she was trying to make a decision. "Well," she decided, "want to go through mine? It's kind of fun."

We all took turns looking at Lee's driver's license. In school, everyone got a kick out of passing her license around. The BCAA got Lee on a bad day. The man who had taken her picture hadn't liked her enough to let her do a redo. She looked high—her eyes sleepy, a dopey, open-mouthed grin on her face—but that wasn't even the worst part. Her hair was sky high, static electricity giving it a lift to the roof. It was the *There's Something About Mary* swoop, the gelled bangs like I used to wear in Grade 7 or something.

"You look so bad," Poppy said.

"Thanks," Lee said, snatching it back. It went back behind the plastic sheet in her wallet.

The Tylenol in her purse rattled when she moved it. She changed necklaces, ditching the lock and key for an owl that I recognized.

"Here," she said, pulling out a long knitted scarf. "Do you like this?" she asked Poppy.

"It's fine."

"Then it's yours," she said. "Think of it as a welcome to Victoria gift. Your compensation for taking a daylong bus ride with this weirdo." She jerked her thumb in my direction.

Poppy took it. Her fingers went through the knitted gaps, her hands playing a closed-circuit cat's cradle.

"Hang on," Lee said, taking it back. "It'll look good with your outfit."

She tied it around Poppy's neck, wrapping it in a stylish way. I used to think scarves were just for keeping warm. Pull it up over your mouth and nose in the wind. Who knew they were an accessory?

"What else do you have in there?" Poppy asked her. She put her hand to her neck. Feeling the weight of the scarf there. Something new.

"I'm kind of using it as an overnight bag. Just enough to get me to Lethbridge to bring Hunter back."

"Oh, yeah?" I asked, widening the opening. I found a few balled-up pairs of socks in there, the lacey edge of a pair of underwear, and a shirt rolled into a sausage. I only just stopped myself from taking out the underwear.

"Bring him back for what?" Poppy asked.

"What?" Lee asked, pretending she hadn't heard.

"You said, so you could bring Hunter back to Victoria. Bring him back for what?"

Lee made eye contact with me over Poppy's head. My lips tightened. My head shook just the tiniest amount. A silent, *Please don't tell her*.

Lee looked down at her purse again. Her hand went down to her chest, to the owl necklace hanging there.

"Hunter gave this to me for my birthday once," she said.

I remembered. I bought it for her from a jewelry store in the mall, borrowed fifty bucks from my dad. She didn't wear it often. Maybe a couple of times a year. When she'd show up at school with it sitting at the center of her sweater, I knew it was going to be a good day. Nothing could go wrong with a sign like that.

"How old were you?" Poppy asked, suddenly curious.

"Grade 10, maybe," she said. "When we'd just started dating." She held it between her hands, the beginning of another cat's cradle. "There was this owl that used to hang around my house. In the backyard. It came out at night, about the same time as my curfew. Hunter's cue to go home, hey? Hunter was always going, 'Man, that owl must hate me. He's kicking me out.'"

My eyes crinkled. I hated that owl. It would let out that eerie hoot right in the middle of a good make-out session and, two seconds later, Lee's dad would call out the window and tell Lee to come inside.

"So he bought you an owl necklace?" Poppy was underwhelmed.

"It was like our little joke," Lee said. She unclasped the necklace and put her hands out to Poppy. Poppy pulled away, just a little, but she didn't stop Lee from putting the necklace around her neck. Clasping it at the back.

Lee's voice got quiet. "Ask Hunter why we're going," she said. "It's his reason for going back. Not mine."

Poppy examined the necklace. I looked out the window. Avoiding eye contact, avoiding the subject, avoiding everything. I leaned my head against the window and watched the blur of the outside flying past me.

The day I was released from hospital, Dad drove me home, patted me on the shoulder, and went back to ignoring things. Mom sat me down at the table and we talked about what was going to keep me a busy little bee for my week of recovery, before the last three weeks of school. All of summer stretching empty out in front of me.

Bridget gave us something to focus on for the next few weeks. She got a phone call from a friend at the beginning of July and decided to go to Vancouver to temp for a month, before the two of them flew to Australia. It felt permanent. Like a real decision. Over dinner, we were all plastic smiles and shoveling our food away, and making conversation about Byron Bay and the Gold Coast and Ayers Rock.

"Do you think I'll find a job there?" Bridget asked, half-and-half pizza open on the table.

"I don't know, hon," Mom said.

"You got a work visa, Bridge. You better be able to find a job."

She rolled her eyes and kicked me under the table.

"I'm sure you'll find something," Mom said.

Dad watched us like a tennis match, moving his eyes back and forth, back and forth. Poor Bridge was going to get to Australia and wonder what the hell Dad was on during her last week home. He didn't know how to talk to me. He wasn't even trying.

"You'll waitress the hell out of Australia," I told her, "at the very least."

"Hunter," Mom said.

By August, Bridget was busy packing and saying goodbye to friends, and making last-minute runs to the store with Mom to pick up toothpaste and flip-flops. Mom and Dad took turns screening my calls—the ones from Josh—and kept the portables downstairs. No visitors until they figured I'd got myself sorted out. Mom sat in my room in the afternoons, waiting patiently for me to talk about what led to my decision to take a whole handful of pills at Bridget's empty apartment. I stayed zipped-up about seeing Niall in that hospital room. One word about it and I knew I'd come undone.

Bridget and me had a heart-to-heart on the last night she was in town. She sat up with me on the couch with the TV on, the neon light on our faces and hands. Her luggage was lined up in the hallway, two giant red suitcases that were heavy even before she packed them full of clothing. The TV screen was making the Northern Lights against the wall behind them, dancing all over the place.

"You doing okay?" she asked me.

"I'm doing fine."

"What do you want to happen next?" she asked me.

"I have no idea."

I stopped on CNN. There was too much on the screen. The scrolling banner at the bottom running through the most recent news, the two people video-conferencing in the middle, a graph on the side. Bounced my eyes around.

"You'll call me in Vancouver? If you need to talk?"

"Yeah," I said. "I'll do that."

Bridget fell asleep on the couch. It was funny, but I hadn't thought even a little bit about the fact that she was going to be on the other side of the world pretty soon. She had been spending the last couple of weeks at home, her apartment downtown empty and ready to be rented to someone else. I didn't think I'd believe in it until she was actually gone. It was her last night home, so I pulled out the pillow from the couch and fell asleep there, too, the light from the TV aurora-borealising around the room.

In the morning, Bridget went to the airport. I went to my room. The phone rang downstairs and no one picked it up.

At the end of August, when I told Mom and Dad that I wasn't going back to school, Dad decided I was going to live with his sister, my Aunt Lynne, in Alberta. A province away. I didn't even complain. I just let Mom do my packing for me. I let Dad drive me through the mountains. I let Aunt Lynne set up everything for me in that new place. I let everything happen.

Why would I want to stay in Victoria, where the ocean that had swallowed Niall waved at me from every direction?

The drive with Dad from Victoria to Lethbridge blurred by. I was zoned-out all the way through the mountains. Alberta was flat and dry. My skin felt tight over my face. It said a lot that I didn't care where I was, because anywhere was better than home.

After Dad left, Aunt Lynne gave me a tour of her single-woman-living house. Couch angled to the TV, remote control on the coffee table. In the fridge was a pathetic tub of margarine, half a block of cheese, and a Styrofoam take-out container. I wondered how long it would take her to send me back to Victoria.

"Help yourself to anything," she said, doing her impression of put-together person.

I left my face in a mask.

"Sure. Thanks."

She ended the tour by showing me the stairs to the basement, wood with carpet slapped on.

"I thought you'd like to be downstairs," she said. "That way, you can have more privacy."

If Dad knew she was giving me a floor to myself, he'd

lose his shit. I figured he wanted me living with Aunt Lynne because she worked at home half the time and could keep an eye on me. Make sure I didn't off myself on her watch. Instead, she was giving me privacy. She didn't seem to know that my privacy privileges had been revoked.

"There's a bathroom down the hall," Aunt Lynne said, switching on lights as we walked through the basement. "Your bedroom is in here." She went upstairs to order a pizza and give me time to unpack my fat duffel.

The room wasn't bad. The half-sized basement windows were depressing and covered with slotted blinds, and a double bed was pushed against the wall. The duvet was forest green and brand new. It had that plastic smell, bought and unwrapped and unused.

I unzipped my bag. I dug around for a clean shirt and put it on. A trio of white envelopes perched on top of all my clothes, my name written in Mom's, Dad's, and Bridget's writing. I didn't feel like reading their optimistic bullshit. Keep your head up. Make the most out of this opportunity. This will be good for you. I put them in the top drawer, flaps sealed, and kicked my bag behind the door.

I'd unpack the rest when I knew how long I was staying for.

I sunk into the bed and dropped my head on the pillow. The ceiling was good. It had a curlicue pattern—stucco and paint—that would work for staring practice. My ceiling at home was flat and white. This was a regular Rorschach test. Whatever Mom and Dad had worked out with Aunt Lynne had been kept confidential. Top secret. Maybe all I'd be doing in Alberta was taking in the ceiling.

"Hunter, are you finished down there?" Aunt Lynne called down the stairs.

Or maybe not.

I went back up.

"Can you set the table?" she said, gesturing at the cupboards. It was a question that didn't sound like a question.

"I thought you were ordering in."

"I am," she said. "But we can still sit down together."

Aunt Lynne wasn't the way I remembered her. The last time we got together was a couple of Christmases ago when she flew out to Victoria and stayed at a hotel downtown. Since then, she'd joined the twenty-first century. She'd stopped wearing old-lady clothes, knits and felted sweaters, subbing out Sears for J. Crew, Banana Republic. She was standing in the kitchen in a purple skirt and black sweater. She'd left her boots on, brown leather up her shins.

Even her hair had lost its Bride-of-Frankenstein frizz. It was like she had stopped trying to look like a Grade 1 teacher, losing the piano-key earrings, the rainbow-toe socks, the weird jewelry she used to pin to the front of her sweater.

We ate our Pizza Hut pizza when it came to the door, complete with two cans of Coke and garlic bread sticks.

"How are you recovering from everything?" Aunt Lynne asked.

She meant my pill overdose. I wished Dad was there for that. I would've killed to see the expression on his face when

Aunt Lynne asked about my attempt. Other than Bridge, no one had asked me directly about that day.

"It was dicey right after," I told her. "I couldn't eat much."

"And now?"

I wolfed down another piece of pizza and hoped she got the message.

"I made you an appointment to see a doctor," she said. She'd let her pizza slice flop sideways on her plate. "Once a month while you're here. Your parents and I think it's good to have someone monitoring you."

"I've been fine," I said.

The pizza was seriously skimping on the toppings. Half a slice of pepperoni and a scrawny mushroom hung out on my slice.

"Hunter, what do you think you're doing here?" she said, suddenly serious.

"Getting out of Dodge," I said. I tried to grin, but the stringy cheese got in my way.

"Look," she said. "I'm not your parents or your sister. I wasn't there when it happened."

"Neither were they."

"But I love you just as much as they do. I think getting out of town for a little while is a good thing for you."

"Change of scenery," I said.

Aunt Lynne put her elbows on the table, her fingers tented together.

"This isn't a vacation," she said. "This is living a normal life. You are going to take care of yourself, and that includes seeing a doctor on a regular basis. You're going to help me around the house and with yard work. You're going to go to school."

"No way," I said quickly.

"Hunter."

"No," I said. "I am not going to some shitty high school just because you think it's a good idea."

She tucked her hair behind her ears, readying herself for Round Two. Firing Squad B. I didn't give her a chance. I got up from the table and went out the back door. I gave it a slam. A nice punch.

I started walking up the alley, gravel crunching under my shoes. I crossed the street and went up the next alley, and then the next. But then I thought about Aunt Lynne, back at her house. What would it look like if I took off on the first night I was there? Besides, I didn't know Aunt Lynne's address, and I wasn't planning on getting lost in some redneck town the first night I got there.

After opening the gate into the backyard, I settled for sitting on the back porch.

Aunt Lynne lived in an ordinary neighborhood, rows of houses with an alley at the back. The house across the alley was two stories with the windows lit up inside. The yellow light made a happy face, two eyes, a nose, and a grinning mouth. Through a bottom window, I could see a girl sitting at a table with her legs pulled up and crossed campfire style. One hand was propping up her chin and the other was holding a pencil.

The back door creaked open. Aunt Lynne sat down beside me on the cement, and all I could think was, Oh, that's why she kept her boots on. Maybe she knew I was a runner before I did.

"Who's that?" I asked her, pointing at the house across the alley.

"Poppy Haynes," she said.

She looked young. Her hair was loose and long, with bangs cut straight across her forehead. They were little-kid bangs. She stretched out one of her crossed legs under the table, like she was shaking out the pins and needles.

"You know, she's homeschooled," Aunt Lynne said. "When I said you should try to do things the way you normally would, I wasn't thinking."

"Normal didn't really work out for me," I said.

"I think maybe we should try something different," she said. "This isn't Victoria. You're not my son, you're my nephew. Maybe school doesn't have to mean a public high school."

She dropped her arm around my shoulder and squeezed. I shrugged her off, just for a sec. It felt too friendly. Like something Niall would do. But Aunt Lynne put her arm right over my shoulder again. This time I left it.

"Are you staying out here for a while?" she asked me.

I nodded my head.

Instead of going back into the kitchen, Aunt Lynne stayed right where she was. It pulled at my chest, her sticking around like that. It gave me a feeling I wanted to memorize like my favorite song.

"We'll get through this," she said. "You're going to be fine."

A week later, Aunt Lynne woke me up from the first real dream I'd had in months. Shaking my shoulder and calling my name. I opened my eyes and it was gone.

I couldn't remember a thing about it, except that it had been there.

"Hunter," she said. "I thought you set an alarm. It's after eight."

"I never wake up this early," I said, sitting up in the bed. The green sheets were wrapped around my body. I was rolled up tight, pig in a blanket. A watery light slanted through the blinds, but it was mostly dark in the basement room. I could spend all day in there and barely know noon from midnight.

"You do now," she said. "Come on. If you want to eat breakfast, you better get moving."

I heard her footsteps on the stairs and then the sound of plates clinking in the kitchen. That sound signaled the end of my weeklong vacation.

I was sleeping well at Aunt Lynne's. In Victoria, I'd given up on sleep. There was only so long I was cool with tentacling my arms and legs out like an octopus in bed, flailing around from side to back to stomach to side all night until I passed out from exhaustion in the morning. Here, it was head-hit-the-pillow sleep, which had a lot to do with how Aunt Lynne had slapped a handyman sticker onto my shirt and given me a to-do list a couple of pages long. I'd been raking up leaves, cleaning out the gutters, painting the back fence, and cleaning out the garage. I had thick calluses on my palms made out of popped and popped-again blisters. I was Stanley Yelnats from *Holes*, without the happy ending.

"I picked up some more cereal," Aunt Lynne said, lining up four boxes on the kitchen counter. Mini Wheats, Raisin Bran, Honey Crisp, and Cheerios. I reached for the Mini Wheats and filled up a bowl. We were relying hard on take-out, but Aunt Lynne had started a grocery list and taped it to the fridge.

"When you're finished, we're going next door," she said. "You can meet Mrs. Haynes and her daughter Poppy. Be your usual happy Hunter self, because you're going to be seeing a lot of them."

"My happy self?" I said, using the cereal bowl like a mug and drinking the rest of the milk.

"Pretend you are going to be here forever," she said. "Put down some roots. Don't burn bridges."

She shot her advice using bullet points. Bang bang bang. Machine-gun fire.

"Try," she said. "And brush your teeth."

I checked my breath in a cupped hand cave, breathing into the hollow.

I'd been in Lethbridge for a week, but Aunt Lynne hadn't given me much of a chance to leave the radius of her house and yard. I'd been to the grocery store with her once, walking down the long aisles and nodding my head when she asked if I'd eat yogurt, chicken, broccoli. Into the cart they'd go. Twice I'd sat in the car with the radio blaring while she ran into the Chinese or Indian place downtown to get us our ordered-out dinner. Other than that, I'd been housebound. An inside dog.

"Last thing," Aunt Lynne said, standing at the front door, hand on the doorknob. "There is no Mr. Haynes, so don't mention him. Don't ask about him. I've known Mrs. Haynes and her daughter since I moved here, and I've seen what they've had to go through over the last year. Poppy's dad is not around. You need to know that."

"I won't say anything."

My aunt left her hand on the doorknob and gave me a look.

"I won't say a word," I said again.

Satisfied, Aunt Lynne opened the door and ushered me through. We crossed the alley.

If there was one thing about Lethbridge that I loved, it was that it was far away from the ocean. The smell of the air was pure prairie. Not a hint of salt water. The wind was bone dry. It sucked the spit off my teeth and left me winded.

The house behind Aunt Lynne's was a little bigger, a little neater, and depressing as hell. Mrs. Haynes was compensating with her outfit, one of those matching three-pieces: pink shirt, pink jacket, pink blouse underneath.

"You must be Hunter," she said, taking my hand with two of hers.

"Hi, Mrs. Haynes." I was expecting her to say, "No, please call me Jackie or Samantha or Mary or Trish." But she left it formal.

"Poppy's in the living room. Why don't you go and introduce yourself."

We split ways, Mrs. Haynes and my aunt forking off into the kitchen, while I wandered down a hallway to the living room. A flat screen was mounted on the wall and a giant kitchen-table-sized coffee table was in the middle of the room. Poppy, with her straight bangs and her knees pulled up to her chin, sat on a couch under the rectangular window. I plopped down beside her. A small gray cat named Gregory hung around the house. When he jumped up on the couch, I patted him from head to tail.

"Hey," I said. "I'm Hunter."

"I'm Poppy," she said.

Her hair was pulled into a high ponytail. She reminded me of a horse, a tiny pony at someone's farm. She had a couple of Band-aids on her arm, the gross skin-colored ones that look like leprosy.

It only took a couple of seconds with her to know what the Band-aids were for. The kid wouldn't leave her arms alone. She scratched at them with her short and stubby nails, working away at a piece of her wrist. I wanted to pull her hand away. I wanted to put a pair of gloves on her, the human equivalent of how you stop a dog from chewing at his paws. Put socks on him.

"Do you like homeschooling?" I asked her. She looked at me then for the first time. Before, she'd been staring straight ahead, not even using her peripherals. Now she turned head-on. Her eyes were dark brown and flanked by the longest lashes.

Gregory leapt from my lap to hers.

Traitor.

"It's okay," she said. "It's better than going to normal school." Poppy reached for the remote. "Want to watch TV? They might be a while."

"Sure."

After that, me and Poppy got into a routine of homeschool at her house. Her mom, call-me-Mrs.-Haynes, was the timekeeper, switching our subjects after an hour. We were in a perfect rotation of Language Arts, Social Studies, Science, and Math.

One week of being homeschooled made me realize that learning is only a tiny piece of school. Most of school is about what goes on while the teacher isn't looking, about the people you're trying to avoid, or the people you're trying to spend more time with. Take that away and I guess you really do learn something.

Poppy scratched at the checkerboard of Band-aids up and down her arms while she did her work, without even seeming to notice she was doing it.

A week of being homeschooled made it routine, and I broke that routine when Aunt Lynne made me take a morning off to see a doctor.

"The doctor at home didn't say anything about getting checked-up," I told Aunt Lynne while we drove to the clinic.

"Well, Google says you can have complications from a pill overdose," she said, honking at a red Chevy that cut her off. "Kidney failure, liver problems, respiratory and circulatory issues."

"Yeah, I'm not having any of those," I said. "Picture of health."

"Humor me," she said, before laying on the horn again.

She stayed in the waiting room while I stripped to my boxers, was weighed, measured, poked, and prodded. When we left, I was minus four vials of blood and had a scratchy throat. I swear, maybe you don't go into the doctor's office sick, but you always come out of it with a cold.

"Can I maybe skip homeschool today?" I asked her.

Aunt Lynne snorted. "No, Hunter," she said. "You cannot skip homeschool."

She dropped me off at the Haynes's and parked in her alley driveway. I gave her a wave, just the tiniest turn of my palm. She waved back and went inside to meet her music students.

Aunt Lynne taught piano in the front room of her house. When I was home in the evenings, I helped out with the door, ushering in six-year-olds to seventy-year-olds while the latest lesson was finishing up. I didn't mind hearing teenagers polishing up concert pieces. The worst was listening to the kids clunking out scales for the first time.

"Hey, Pops," I said, when she let me into the house. The nickname just slipped out of my mouth.

"How was your appointment?" she asked.

"Healthy as a horse," I said, winking.

Poppy wasn't even a teenager yet. Grade 7 and there was something pretty little-kid about her. Maybe it was because she didn't dress like a hipster. Long-sleeved shirt, jeans, and no jewelry. It made her look out of touch.

"Mom didn't think you were coming back after lunch," she said, "so she didn't leave anything."

"She's not here?"

Poppy shook her head.

"Hey, Greg," I told the cat, bending down to pick him up. He always slunk in on a ten-second delay. "Gregory looks like he could use some fresh air." I looked up at Poppy. "How about you?"

"You want to leave?" she asked me.

"Sure," I said. "I haven't seen much of Lethbridge. You want to show me around?"

Poppy tipped her head to the side, giving me the old once-over. My jeans that hugged my calves, looking more like girl jeans than hers did. My zipped hoodie over a t-shirt.

"Do I need a haircut or something?" I asked her. She shook her head. Then she went to the closet and returned with a pair of shoes and a sweater.

"I have to put Gregory in the bathroom," she said. "He's not allowed to have the run of the house."

"Don't do that," I said. "We'll take him with us."

While Poppy got her shoes on, I took a quick look around the boot room. I found some twine on a spool, and I measured it out and tied it around Gregory's collar. If Lee were here, she'd laugh her ass off. "Hunter Ryan," she'd say. "That is ridiculous."

"You can't walk a cat," Poppy said. "It's embarrassing."

"So?" I said. "I don't know anyone here."

I waited outside while Poppy locked up the house. Gregory went exploring, checking out the bushes along the driveway. I kept expecting him to lift his leg like a dog and leave his mark.

"Be a man, Gregory," I told him.

We walked away from Poppy's house and down the residential street. It was that late September weather that is halfway between Indian summer and fall. Cold in the shade, hot in the sun. It felt good to be walking instead of sitting shotgun in Aunt Lynne's car. Walking around made it easier to memorize our location.

"Is there a fast-food place around here?" I asked Poppy. She stayed a couple of steps ahead of me. Lee used to do that when she was mad at me. She'd stay one sidewalk square ahead of me and never let me catch up.

"There's a Dairy Queen," she said.

"You want to lead the way?"

Poppy did. She didn't say much. Like when we sat at the big table together at her house, working on Math, and I'd try and crack a joke. She didn't give away a smile, not even a hint of her teeth showing. I had to work hard to impress her.

"Did you ever go to school?" I asked her.

Poppy's shoulders stiffened. I'd surprised her out of her fast way of walking. She slowed right down and came into line with me and Gregory.

"Yeah," she said. "I just started homeschooling last year."

"No way," I said. "I kind of figured you'd always been homeschooled."

"No," she said. "Here, we're passing my old school."

The two-story middle school took up most of the block. Poppy walked by it without turning her head. It wasn't much to look at. A school is a school is a school. There was a line of cars parked out front and the bell rang as we walked past.

"Hurry up," Poppy said, picking up her pace.

We didn't talk much until we got to the Dairy Queen. It didn't take more than twenty minutes to walk there, but twenty minutes of silence is a lot of quiet.

"You can't bring the cat in," Poppy told me, looking pointedly at Gregory.

"Shhh," I said, covering his cat ears. "Don't let him hear you."

Poppy rolled her eyes and I'd never felt so uncool. A twelve-year-old thought I was cheesing up the place.

"Look, take this." I handed over a twenty-dollar bill. Aunt Lynne had paid me for my hard work around the house, making it a little bit better than child labor. "Get anything you want as long as you get me an Oreo Blizzard. A big-daddy large one."

Poppy made a face. Then she turned around and went into the DQ. Waiting for her to pick up our orders, I took Gregory for a walk around the parking lot. It wasn't until I was a couple of feet away from the entrance that I picked up on that oh-so-familiar smell of someone smoking up.

I followed my nose to the alley behind the DQ, where a couple of kids a little younger than me were leaning on the fence, Jordan Catalano style, and passing around a joint. You'd think I wouldn't be stupid enough to search for drugs just a couple of months after an overdose. But weed wasn't pills.

"Is that cat on a leash?" asked a kid who was probably

Poppy's age but looked a lot older.

"Pass me that joint and I'll let you take him around the block," I said.

The kids laughed, begrudgingly widening their circle and letting me in.

"So where can I get a little more of this?" I asked. "I just moved here."

One of the kids gave me an address that I'd be following later, a little Alice in Wonderland and down the rabbit hole. I tried not to think about how creepy I looked, towering over a group of preteens.

I was still back there when Poppy started calling my name, walking around the corner in time to see me chummy with a bunch of kids like her. For a second, I figured she'd be happy to see some people close to her age. The expression on her face flickered between a smile and a frown. When she didn't come further into the alley, I moved toward her, Gregory in tow.

"Hey, thanks," I told her. "Thanks, Pops."

Poppy shoved my Blizzard into my chest and walked away.

"What'd you get?" I asked her, but I was addressing her back.

Behind me, the kids laughed.

"See you later, Poppy," one of them yelled, the one who had provided me with an address.

I scooped up Gregory and turned back onto the sidewalk, following Poppy's sweater. Maybe Poppy knew one of the guys in the alley and she wanted to avoid him.

"Hey," I said, catching up to her. "What'd you get at DQ?"

"Nothing," she said. "I wasn't hungry."

"Do you know those guys back there?"

Poppy took Gregory out of my hands and pulled him to her chest.

"No," she said. "And neither do you."

Then she speed-walked out of there, leaving me behind. It took me half an hour to get home. I couldn't remember the way back.

One Saturday morning, Aunt Lynne came downstairs, phone in hand. She was still in her pajamas, striped white and blue from the Gap.

"Hunter, you have a phone call," she said and, from the smile on her face, I knew it wasn't from my parents.

"Hello?"

I had early morning voice, froggy croak sending me back to puberty.

"Hunter," Penner said, his voice practically gleeful on the other line. "It's nice to talk to you."

"Don't make it sound like I'm your girlfriend, Penner," I told him. "Technically, I don't have to talk to you anymore. I'm not a student. As the police would say, I'm no longer under your jurisdiction."

Leave it to me to crack up the old guy over the phone. He cackled out a laugh.

"I've missed our weekly meetings," he said.

It was different talking to him on the phone. It felt like he had a direct line to my brain, straight to the center of my head.

"How are you adjusting to Alberta?"

"Well, shit, Penner, what do you think?"

"What do I think?" Penner said, making it purposefully abstract. "I think taking a step away from the situation, and from Victoria, is probably a step in the right direction."

"You don't think it's running away?" I asked him.

It was something Mom had said. That leaving BC was running away from my problems.

"No," Penner said, definitively. "Is there anything in Victoria for you right now?"

"My parents," I said.

"And?"

"My parents," I repeated.

"And what's in Alberta?"

Who knew why, but Poppy's little face popped into my head at just that moment. Wearing her kid bangs and shoving my Blizzard into my chest. She had used some serious force on that.

"I don't know yet," I said. I waited a beat and then said, "Anybody miss me?"

"I'm not going to talk about here," Penner said. "How about you tell me how you've been adjusting."

"I made a friend," I said.

"Good for you," Penner said.

"Yeah, she's my twelve-year-old neighbor."

He kept me on the phone for half an hour. I guess between the two types of meetings I'd had with Penner—in person and over the phone—I liked the second one better. I spent at least half of the time in Penner's office trying to avoid making direct eye contact with him. Over the phone, I didn't have that problem. Even though Penner wouldn't talk much about what was happening back in Victoria, he still served as an anchor back to there. Making it so I couldn't get away from home that easily. For the first time since I'd come to live with Aunt Lynne, I thought seriously about what I'd left behind.

By the time Penner hung up, satisfied with our progress, I was wide awake and ready for the day. I took the phone back upstairs to Aunt Lynne.

"Hang on to that," she said. "Call your parents first and then your sister second. They forwarded her number in Australia."

"I'm not calling Bridge," I said. "I don't want to cramp her Australian style."

"Call them," she said. "And then we're meeting Poppy and her mom for brunch at IHOP. Get moving, Hunter."

"Jesus," I said, exhaling. "Tall order."

I did Aunt Lynne's bidding, dialing home first, Bridget after. Two more anchors that secured me to Victoria. Mom and Dad tiptoed around me, mostly giving me a pie-chart rendering of their week: hours spent watching TV, working, and exercise. Bridget was better because she had middle ground to talk about, somewhere that was neither Victoria nor Lethbridge. There was still something that felt like walking on eggshells about our conversation. As if Bridget had a list, ten items long, of the subjects she could talk to me about. We all stayed pretty surface-level. I was emptied out at the end of it, tipped over and drained out.

Aunt Lynne watched me over her coffee cup, pretending to read the paper. I wondered what it sounded like to her, my one side of the phone call.

"Ten minutes, Hunter," she said. "Then we should go."

I headed to the basement to change into a clean shirt and jeans.

Maybe Aunt Lynne knew what she was doing by keeping me too busy to think. Because when I was downstairs with no more phone calls to wade through, my present situation became a little clearer. Me here in Lethbridge, and Mom, Dad, and Bridget somewhere else. I had that desert island feeling, alone with my SOS, trying to flag down help. I lay down on my bed and didn't get up. My limbs were heavy. They were weighted by the Mafia and sunk down to the bottom of the ocean. My cement shoes. My handcuffed arms.

Aunt Lynne didn't come to get me when it was time to leave. She left it in my hands to finally drag my ass out of bed, step into my shoes, and follow her out to the car.

We were late for brunch. The IHOP parking lot was packed and Aunt Lynne had to squeeze between two SUVs. Aunt Lynne did the frantic look-around-the-restaurant when we got there. Poppy and her mom were in a corner booth. I sat beside Poppy, and I must've looked in poor form because she didn't give me any shit for the day before.

"Hey," she said.

I gave her a nod. My mouth was sandpaper dry.

Poppy's hair was up in a ponytail again, swinging gently as she examined the menu. Aunt Lynne and Mrs. Haynes were talking reality TV, while me and Poppy studied our menus as if we were preparing for the next exam.

"What are you getting?" she asked me.

I shrugged my shoulders.

"I'm not hungry."

Poppy's eyebrows shot up and she aimed a glare in my direction.

"This was my mom's idea," she whispered. "No one cares what you get but you better get something."

"Fine," I said. "How about I get what you get."

She turned back to her menu, studying even harder.

In Victoria I went out for brunch plenty. Before I met Niall, me, Josh, and Lee made a cool trio. We would bus downtown and wait in the long, snaky lines at the Blue Fox Cafe until a table freed up. Lethbridge didn't have Victoria breakfast places. An IHOP is an IHOP is an IHOP; it doesn't matter where you are.

Aunt Lynne was watching me from across the table, giving me a look when the waiter came by. Poppy ordered herself a stack of Tutti Frutti pancakes, and I matched her order like I said I would. She hid a grin in her orange juice. We spent the rest of breakfast doing the mazes and the crossword puzzles on the children's placemats. The crayons were fat and pressed down to stubs. Then we played a game of Hangman. Poppy really put some imagination into her hanging body, adding some blood, a cool top hat, and a pair of laced-up boots every time I guessed a wrong letter.

Maybe that's why I didn't notice it at first. I was too busy sweating about not guessing the right word. It was a funny moment to get lost in, playing kids games with Poppy, jousting with our crayons. But when I finally looked up, right in time for Tutti Frutti delivery, I noticed that we seemed to be the stars of the show. A couple of people were taking these tiny glances at us. Not many of them, just a handful or so, but some were outright staring. Did the four of us look that mismatched? Or was it something else? I hoped my eyes were looking as empty as I'd felt that morning. I looked from person to person, imagining I was Scott Summers with my pair of laser eyes.

"Hey, Pops, how come we have an audience?"

Poppy didn't look up from the table. She gave the hangman a cane. One more incorrectly guessed letter.

"Guess we're pretty popular," she said.

It made me wonder about Poppy and her mom. Her missing, absent dad. The Mr. Haynes who wasn't around.

We finished our breakfast. The Tutti Frutti pancakes were better than I thought they'd be. Even if they had a girly name. When we stood up and put on our jackets, it was our final curtain call. Come on out. Take a bow.

On the Bus

The big sign coming into town said Revelstoke, checking off another stop along the way. We still weren't even halfway to Victoria. It was getting dark outside, December deep, and the tops of the trees got lost in the dark sky.

The bus pulled into town and stopped, letting people on, letting people off, and giving us an hour to stretch our legs and stomachs.

"Bundle up, Pops," I told her. She had this skinny windbreaker on over her sweater. It was Helly Hanson, built for ski season, but it looked too thin for Revelstoke winter. Lee had given her a scarf, and she was going to have to pull it up high out here. There was snow all over the place and it was still lightly falling down. The mountains here just overlapped one another, one after the other after the other, until you didn't know where one stopped and the next one started. I wished I'd told Poppy to bring a hat or something.

Maybe a pair of gloves. I stuffed my hands into my pockets and, once the bus was parked, we headed down the aisle.

The nosy old woman was still sitting in the seat in front of Poppy. I had seen her looking at the three of us, trying to puzzle out how we all fit together. She stayed on the bus when we got off, and I wondered if she was going to spend the entire hour there. She was so curved, her shoulders rounding forward, her neck arching toward the seat in front of her. I thought I was slouched, but I had nothing on this woman.

I had this feeling, while we walked by her, that I should hold Poppy's hand. Make it seem like she really belonged with us. Make believe she was my little sister or something. But the kid was twelve years old, and you stop doing that kind of thing when they're close to middle school. I shadowed Poppy down the aisle, making her one of us.

"I'm setting a timer," Lee said, pushing down on the buttons running on the outside of her watch. "I don't want to miss the bus."

"We're not going to miss it," I told her. The bus was sitting out like a shiny worm, parked right in the middle of everything. If we picked the right restaurant, we could keep an eye out for when people started getting back on while we ate dinner.

"Thought about what you want to eat?" I asked Poppy.

"Anything's good," she said.

"We'll try to find one of those hundred-item-menu places," I said. "Something for everyone."

A few people were bundled on the street, pushing into

restaurants or stores still open. The entire bus was out here, taking a rest from that same seat-studded interior.

I could see a pizza place, an Italian place, and a Tim Hortons from where I was standing. Lee pointed across the street, and it looked like what we needed. Bright fluorescent lights and tables by the window.

I put my arm around Poppy's shoulders. She didn't shrug me off. We went inside this diner-type place that was half-empty.

Half-full, Penner would've corrected me. *Think in terms of optimism*. It was tiring, trying to find the good side of a situation. Sometimes it was better just to slouch into the negative. It was comfy down there.

The three of us had run out of things to say to each other. The menus were good placeholders. Burger or Reuben. Pizza or calzone. Iced tea or Pepsi. I snuck a couple of looks at Lee over the top of my menu. Her mascara had drifted, giving her eyes a bit of a black outline. Her ponytail was falling out, dragging the elastic band down an inch from where it was supposed to be. I wanted to reach over and pull the whole thing out. Hair down and loose and around her shoulders.

Outside, a police car drove by the restaurant, the policeman inside taking a slow look through our window. I bobbed my head instinctively, panic creeping up my chest. Lee and Poppy didn't seem to think anything of it, but I couldn't help but be reminded of Poppy's mom. She would know Poppy was gone by now.

Worrying over the police car made me point randomly at

the menu when the waitress came. Ended up with a salad. I'd never ordered a salad at a restaurant in my life.

Me and Niall used to wander around Victoria after midnight and stop in diners like this when we found them. Niall never ordered anything other than a Diet Coke. Why it was always Diet, I had no idea, but he'd drink glass after glass of it, carbonated bubbles moving up his circus-striped straw. Sometimes you need just one place in the city to be open 24-hours. Easy, anytime access.

We all picked at our food when it came. Poppy dissected her sandwich, eating the meat, then the cheese, then the lettuce, and leaving all the bread.

"That's an interesting way to eat a sandwich," I told her. I stole a couple of fries off her plate. She shoved it across the table.

"Finish it if you're that hungry. Who orders a salad in a diner, anyway?" She got up and headed to the washrooms at the back of the restaurant. Me and Lee exhaled as one as Poppy disappeared. Took away some of the awkwardness between us.

But not all of it.

It wasn't easy silence between us. It was pulled tight as a rope.

"You could've called," I told Lee, saying it quick before Poppy came out of the bathroom. Some people were filing onto the bus. I could see them out the window. Lee paid the bill with her dad's Visa, signing some version of his signature. It didn't matter that the name on the card was a man's name. No one checked that.

Lee waited until the waitress was gone. Then she leaned across the table. Her elbow just missed a blob of spilled ketchup.

"Yeah, like your parents would give me your number," she said.

"Did you try Bridge?"

"Dude, your sister doesn't give a shit. Plus she doesn't live here anymore."

I wanted to correct Lee, to tell her she was wrong. Bridge gave more than a shit about what happened last year.

"How'd you find me, then?"

"Believe it or not, I figured it out through Mr. Penner. I set up an appointment to see him, like you used to every week. He said you were staying in Alberta; he told me the city; I checked out a phone book and found your last name." She touched the sleeve of my sweater, bunching up the fabric. "It was because of Josh. When he said he saw you, I thought, *Why not*? You left. That didn't mean we had to let you go completely."

I shifted my arm, making it so her hand slipped over my palm.

"And you just got on a bus."

"Yeah," she said. "I just got on a bus."

"Why?"

Lee looked down at the sprinkling of crumbs on the table.

"Because I didn't care. Not last year, when you needed someone to. You changed and I couldn't deal with that. There wasn't really a chance for me to take that back. Until I heard about Niall and found out no one had told you."

She held my hand across the table.

Poppy came back from the washrooms and looked at us pointedly.

"We should get going," she said. "Everyone's on the bus."

"Guess we should," I said.

"I ate way too much," Lee said, rubbing her stomach. She heaved herself out of the booth.

"Better that than still hungry." I rubbed my own stomach, emptier than I wanted it to be.

The bus driver announced that we'd be passing through Salmon Arm next. Lee sat across the aisle, leaving two seats for me and Poppy. *Salmon Arm*. I imagined a hundred salmon swimming in the river, touching scales to scales until they formed the shape of a human arm, their pink and orange and gray-colored bodies inching past the town.

"Lee's in a food coma," I told Poppy. It was true. Her head was against the window and her eyes were closed.

The lights in the bus dimmed. The snow outside was swirling in large, snaky movements, wrapping itself along the outside of the bus.

"What are we going to do in Victoria?" Poppy asked me. That came out of left field, a big old baseball thrown unexpectedly to home, taking out the catcher.

"I don't know, Pops."

It occurred to me that I didn't have an idea.

"Well, you should," Poppy said.

Aunt Lynne celebrated my one-month-long stay by buying me one of those cheapo Walmart bookshelves. She found a toolbox in the garage and set me to work putting it together. I was getting a pretty good collection of books from Language Arts classes at Poppy's house. Mrs. Haynes was assigning about a thousand times more reading than I got back in high school, and I'd already read three paperbacks front to back.

"Are you going to give me a hand?" I asked Aunt Lynne.

"Think of it as Shop class," she said. "I'll supervise."

She went back to the newspaper, reading out my weekend horoscope from the D pages. I tuned out like I always did when she started going on about Moons in Venus. It sounded like a Niall thing. Believing in the unbelievable.

Poppy came over when I was halfway through building my bookshelf. I had a bad feeling that I'd built it upside down. I'd have to fit the shelves in backwards or something.

Poppy padded down the stairs like a cat.

"In here," I said, flagging her down with my arm out the doorway of my room.

Poppy leaned against the wall, surveying my bedroom. Her socks were warm and wooly, straight out of Mark's Work Warehouse. I knew because Aunt Lynne had taken me there to do some light shopping and she'd bought me three packs of socks. Me and Poppy could match.

"What's up?" I asked her.

I'm not saying me and Poppy were friends, exactly. Twelve wasn't seventeen and we didn't have a ton in common. What I'm saying is that seeing the same person every day for six hours a day makes you friendly, if not friends.

"There wasn't much going on at my house."

"Join the club," I told her.

"Do you need any help?" she asked.

Poppy picked up my packet of instructions from the floor, Walmart's Rosetta Stone of languages crammed into a ten-page booklet.

"Have at it," I told her.

My knees crunched when I stood up. I plopped onto my bed so Poppy could take my place by the bookshelf. There was just the sound of the tiny pages turning and Poppy's near-silent nose breathing.

"I think you did this wrong," she said.

"I don't care," I said. "Just keep building it wrong."

"Okaaay," she said.

To say that Poppy tinkered would be an understatement. It sounded heavy duty, what she was doing with the bookshelf. I had been all touchy-feely with the wooden shelf, but you could really hear Poppy going to town on that thing. Dad had never been a very hands-on guy around the house, and it wasn't like I'd ever had any interest in Shop class and woodworking.

"I guess I should call you next time I need something put together," I told her. "Where'd you learn to do that?"

"My dad," she said.

Aunt Lynne had been all weird about Poppy's dad. Mr. Haynes is not around. There is no Mr. Haynes. Made it sound like we were in a movie from the future, with Tom Cruise hanging out around the corner and making people disappear. Poppy's voice didn't crackle when she said, "My dad." Either he'd been gone for a long time, or she was just over the fact that he wasn't around anymore.

"Thanks, Poppy's dad," I said out loud.

Poppy's shoulders went still. "It's done, basically," she said. "You just have to glue on this thing."

She waved a wood-colored piece of floppy paper at me.

"I can probably manage that," I said. Glue was not my strong point. I always ended up pasting my thumb to my first finger.

"Want to get out of here for a bit?" I asked Poppy. "We could take Gregory for a walk."

Poppy shrugged her shoulders. "I guess."

"Meet you out front?"

I stood the bookshelf up and pushed it against the wall. I skipped the glue step. I rolled up the wood-colored paper and tossed it into my bathroom trash. Some heavy classical music was coming from upstairs, Aunt Lynne shut into the front room for the afternoon. She'd left a post-it note on the fridge for me.

Don't forget to call Mr. Penner today. I mean it, Hunter.

I balled it up and threw it in the trash. I'd call Penner later. I'd make it go with his after-dinner drink.

"Pops, when did you get a sweater for Gregory?"

The cat was wearing a red and black striped sweater with two leg holes popped out the front. It wasn't cold out— more an accessory than a necessity. Fall had happened in Lethbridge in one day, all of the leaves blowing down off of the trees. It was still blowing. I pulled my hood up over my head.

"Want to come with me on an errand?" I asked Poppy.

What I did next wasn't family approved. Bringing a kid along on a drug deal was not par for the course.

"Where are we going?"

"To my friend's house. I'm just going to pick something up."

"You have a friend?"

Poppy deadpanned it, and I couldn't tell if she was genuinely asking or if she was making fun of me.

"Call it an acquaintance."

I held Gregory's leash. His tail swished back and forth. One difference between Lethbridge and Victoria was that I didn't know anyone in Lethbridge. I was Hunter Anonymous. You wouldn't catch me walking a cat in Victoria, but I didn't give a shit doing it in Lethbridge. Give me fifty cats on leashes and I'd still be cool as a cucumber about it.

There wasn't much traffic on the roads. We had the sidewalk to ourselves, and Poppy was busy avoiding stepping on the cracks. It was tail-end-of-summer weather.

Flicking back and forth in a goodbye.

"I thought Alberta was supposed to be like the arctic," I said. I had to roll up the sleeves of my sweater.

"Sometimes it's warm even in the winter. You haven't heard of Chinooks?"

"No."

"Look it up," Poppy said and walked ahead.

I fiddled around with my phone, checking up on the GPS map that was taking me to the address I'd scored at the DQ. It was twenty minutes away, straight up Thirteenth Street and then hang a left. I used my hand as a visor to shield my phone from the glare of the sun as I did a quick search for "Chinook."

"Oh," I told Poppy. "So a warm wind from the Rocky Mountains."

Poppy elbowed me. "It means snow eater, dude. In Blackfoot."

"Well," I said, skimming the rest of the Wikipedia entry. "You are correct, Pops."

I led the way down a side street. Gregory had his nose to the ground. He reminded me of Sherlock Holmes. All he needed was the jaunty hat.

"Where are you going?" Poppy asked.

"My friend's," I said again.

"This isn't your friend's," she said. "I know where we are."

I parked myself in front of the right house, my GPS dot lining up with my final destination. The houses on this street looked more like Victoria houses, with sunrooms in the front and porches enclosed by glass.

"Nice. So you're a pothead?" Poppy asked me.

"No," I said, defensively. "Why would you think that?"

Poppy jerked her thumb at the house in front of us. "I'm not stupid. I know where we are," she said. "I went to school with the guy who lives here. I know his dad deals."

Then she removed my hand from Gregory's leash and took a step back.

"Hurry up," she said. "We'll wait out here."

I wasn't in the house for more than ten minutes. Fifteen minutes, tops. Just to get what I needed. When I got back outside, Poppy wasn't alone. She was standing with three kids, holding Gregory tightly to her chest. The guy I recognized from the alley a few days before, the one who gave me the address. The two girls were both taller than Poppy, with woolen hats over their loose, long hair. They all shut up and went still the second I walked out.

"Poppy?" I said from the top step of the porch. Walking into the middle of the group crowding her, I said something lame like, "Hey, hey."

"Need your boyfriend to help you out?" one of the girls said.

"He's not my boyfriend," Poppy said.

"Come on," I said to her. "We should go."

Poppy broke out of the tiny circle, holding Gregory closer than ever. When we were far enough away from the house and the kids, I put my hand on Poppy's shoulder. She shrugged it off.

"Do you know them from school?"

"I don't go to school," Poppy said. "Or did you smoke that

important fact out of your head?"

"You used to."

"Yeah, sure," Poppy said. "They were my friends. Things change. Where are all of your friends from school, Hunter? You still close with them?"

Poppy took off, fast-walking and disappearing at the corner. I had to stop and type Aunt Lynne's address back into my GPS.

Maybe Poppy was bullied, and that's why her Mom pulled her out for homeschooling. But Poppy didn't seem like the bullied type.

"Hunter. Doctor," Aunt Lynne said. She shook her keys at me, guiding me toward the door. I scooped up my shoes with the tips of my toes and stepped into them on my way outside.

Aunt Lynne's car still smelled like Chinese food take-out from the night before, when it had sat in the backseat for fifteen minutes while we ran into Shoppers Drug Mart for toothpaste.

I buckled myself in, wincing as Aunt Lynne launched her phone at my junk.

"Call your parents," she said. "They're expecting to hear from you."

"Jesus," I said. "Right now?"

"Yes, Hunter," she repeated. "Right now."

Life with Aunt Lynne was actually turning out okay, even though she didn't let me get away with shit.

I dialed the number home.

"Hey, Mom," I said when she answered. First ring.

"Hunter, how are you?"

"Fine," I said. "Me and Aunt Lynne are on our way to my doctor's appointment. Did she tell you I have to get these check-ups? They take about five vials of my blood, makes me all lightheaded. Maybe you could talk to her and ask her to get off my case."

"Hunter," Aunt Lynne said, her voice criminally level. The clicking sound of the indicator stuck in my head.

"Anyway," I said, aware of the fact that Mom hadn't said anything yet. "Things are good. How are you and Dad?"

Mom filled me in on as much as she could. I could see her skipping over parts and pieces, blacking out large chunks of information. She would've made an awesome censor back in WWII, using a felt marker to black out top-secret information in soldiers' letters home.

"Have you seen Niall?" I asked her.

Mom left a thick silence.

"I have not," she said carefully.

"I didn't think you had," I said. "Just checking. It's nice to know that nothing changes, hey?"

"Okay, Hunter, give me the phone," Aunt Lynne said, reaching across the middle console.

"Pretty sure it's illegal to talk and drive," I told her, keeping the phone just out of reach.

"Wrap it up," she told me, spinning an invisible wheel beside her head.

"We're almost at the doctor's," I told Mom. "I'll call back if they tell me anything serious. How's that sound?"

"We'll talk soon," Mom said.

Aunt Lynne dropped her phone back into her purse at her feet, between the bottom of the seat and the gas and brake pedals. It looked pretty dangerous down there. Every once in a while she'd catch the heel of her shoe in the straps and frantically work at getting untangled before the next red light.

"Well, gee," I said. "I sure feel better after talking to Mom."

"Can it, Hunter," Aunt Lynne said. "You can't just not talk to her the entire time you're living here. I don't care if you talk about world peace or you talk about the weather, you're going to talk to your parents on a regular basis."

"Great," I said.

Aunt Lynne pulled into the parking lot at the clinic and pressed the power locks to let us out. We both went into the clinic together. I wished she'd just let me go in alone. Going in like we were a child/guardian buddy system felt all wrong.

Aunt Lynne took a seat by the window and started flipping through an old copy of *People* magazine. When my name was called, she furtively tore out a page from the middle and stuffed it into her jacket pocket. Then she rode my coattails from the waiting room into the patient rooms in the back.

I'd seen Dr. Griffin a couple of times now. Right off the bat, he gave me a depression inventory. It was this quick list of five questions that mostly focused on how much sleep I got. I couldn't tell you how pleased I was to tell him that I'd probably never slept better in my entire life. Maybe there was something to sleeping in the basement. Something about being your requisite six feet underground to really get a good rest.

Aunt Lynne asked the doctor a few questions. You could tell she'd been doing her Google homework. Who knew trying to commit suicide could lead down such a dangerous path. I mean, if you weren't successful. Aunt Lynne asked him if he could do some extra blood work. He agreed. He was an old guy with a walrus moustache. Gray hair sprouting from his ears. He was probably five years past retirement, still working hard for his access to the sample medication.

I zoned out and looked over at the cotton swabs and wooden tongue depressors. The box of rubber gloves and the safe-needle deposit.

I let Aunt Lynne lead the way to the east side of the clinic, where they took their five vials and shipped them off to the lab at the hospital. I got that Aunt Lynne was trying to teach me something here. Something about learning the repercussions of your actions. But there wasn't really a repercussion. My liver hadn't failed. My lungs hadn't shriveled up and died. I was pretty much a normal human teenage boy. Adults got off on teaching lessons to kids. But sometimes there wasn't a lesson to learn. Sometimes stuff just happened and you dealt with it. It wasn't all a teachable moment.

But I did it anyway and hoped she'd give up soon.

Aunt Lynne dragged me down to the Salvation Army. For a woman who made a killing through the trifecta of teaching piano lessons, reaping the royalties on her old piano recordings, and working part-time as an elementary school music teacher, she sure liked the secondhand stores. Secondhand books, used clothing, scratched records. She bought a lamp for the living room.

"So, not a complete write-off of a day," Aunt Lynne said, as we pulled back into the driveway. Home again, home again.

I looked toward Poppy's house. I saw her skinny silhouette in the window, reading a book. I carried the lamp under my armpit like a football.

"Not completely," I said.

The next day, I crossed the back alley to Poppy's house, where the car was idling in the driveway, Poppy riding shotgun and Mrs. Haynes fiddling around with the heat. Scrape marks were visible on the windshield where Mrs. Haynes had pulled the scraper back and forth to get rid of the frost.

In Victoria, Lee used to show up at my house on the coldest mornings to give me a ride to school. She always left too late to get the scraping in, and would show up with her face behind a wall of pale blue. Just the tiniest circle scraped for her to see out of.

"Brrrr," I said, knocking Poppy on the elbow. "It's freezing out there."

"It always snows at the end of October," Mrs. Haynes responded. "Takes us all by surprise."

The fur-lined hood of Mrs. Haynes's jacket peeked over the headrest. I pulled my windbreaker across my chest. Eventually the heat kicked in.

It turned out snow in October was not the big surprise of the century. I was more amazed that the homeschooling kids got together for field trips. I thought the reason for being homeschooled was to stay home.

Aunt Lynne had filled me in. She did a quick Google Map of Fort Whoop-Up, where we'd be going, and told me a bit about it so I wouldn't look like a complete tool in front of all the other shut-ins. It was this old fort by the Old Man River that used to be a trading post during the fur trade. Panning for gold. That shit. We were getting a special tour, courtesy of the Lethbridge School Board.

Poppy put her feet up on the dashboard while we drove down the hill beside a Wendy's fast-food restaurant. The high-level bridge arched across the coulees. The closest thing Victoria had to that was the Johnson Street Bridge, old and blue. But this thing was high. It was tip-your-head-back-and-look-up. Made my hands sweaty to actually think about getting in a train and riding across there.

Poppy turned the music up loud on the radio while we drove down the hill and passed under the bridge. Ear-splitting loud. The weird thing was, Mrs. Haynes didn't say a word about it. Poppy was blasting classic rock at the highest volume the radio could go. My heartbeat had worked its way up into my eardrums and was pounding back there for a while. Poppy's hand was gripping the door handle. I could see the bones of her knuckles through her skin.

At the bottom of the hill, Mrs. Haynes pulled into the parking lot outside the fort. She turned down the music and Poppy was dead quiet. She got out of the car and waited for me by the headlights.

"Thanks for the ride," I told Mrs. Haynes.

"It's no problem, Hunter. I'll be back in two hours to pick you both up."

"Hope your ears aren't ringing too bad," I said, making a joke out of Poppy's music. But Mrs. Haynes didn't laugh. She barely cracked a smile. She waited for me to get out of the car before she backed out of the parking lot and headed back up the hill.

I followed Poppy into the fort. Forty kids were crowded into the center courtyard. Me and Poppy were the oldest by far. These kids were eight and ten years old, not even close to leaving elementary school. Maybe Poppy looked like she belonged, almost, but I looked like someone you wanted to keep your children away from. I could almost see the parent chaperones stepping between me and everybody else, forming a wall against the seventeen-year-old high school guy.

Poppy grinned, her first of the morning.

"You think it's funny?" I asked her. "It won't be when they cart me off to jail as the creeper who tags along on homeschooling field trips. Then you'll be stuck here by yourself."

"Sounds okay, actually," Poppy said. "Sort of like something I'd pay to see."

She pulled her hat firmly over her ears and led the way to

check-in with the chaperones. Our parent chaperone was a fat woman in a shapeless winter jacket. She had a pair of cat ears attached to her head with a hairband. The Goth trend finally permeating parent culture.

"Poppy Haynes and Hunter Ryan," Poppy said. She announced our names like we were important people. Introducing Lord and Lady. Announcing the arrival of.

"I was told you two would be coming," the woman said, bobbing her head down to her attendance sheet. She had a lemon expression on her face, pinched at the corners of her mouth. Her lips turned down. The way she looked at Poppy, you'd think she was the son of Satan. The Antichrist in the flesh.

"Your ears are falling off," I told the woman.

"Oh," she said, fixing her headband. No "thank you." She took a step back from both of us. I could tell she wanted one of those Avian flu masks that you pick up for airplane travel. She acted as if we were contagious.

"Hey," I told her, feeling mean, "you should lose the costume."

"It's our Halloween-themed field trip. We like to keep it festive for the kids. The two of you were welcome to dress up," she said, turning her back to us.

"Well, shit," I said to Poppy when the woman was gone. "Guess we should've dressed up, hey? Even though we got about a week to go before it's actually Halloween."

Poppy nudged me with her shoulder, encouraging me to take a look around the fort. She was right. Cat Ears wasn't the only one dressed for the occasion. Most of the parent chaperones had something marking them as cool with the holiday. A witch hat. A pair of angel wings with the too-tight elastic bands that turned their arms into sausages. Cowboy boots.

That last one might have just been Alberta.

"I don't want to do this tour," Poppy said. "Come on. We're signed in. Want to just wander around the park until Mom picks us up?"

I followed her back out the gates. We had never actually belonged on the field trip. Who knew how Mrs. Haynes and Aunt Lynne had decided it would be a good idea for us to go. Poppy was being slippery, sneaking around with her body all elastic and camouflaged against the building. I didn't know where we were going. All I knew was that Poppy had a thing about the high-level bridge. Every time we went by it together, she'd do that trick with the music. Turn it up sky high and blast our eardrums. Now Poppy was leading us away from it and away from the fort.

I didn't think we were going to do anything for Halloween next week. I didn't even remember seeing a box of mini-chocolate bars around the house. Who knew what Aunt Lynne was planning on handing out to the kids.

I'd had a good Halloween the year before. It had just been me and Niall, and we had taken two boxes of Halloween candy down to the beach. We got a little high and snacked ourselves silly. I picked out all the Snickers bars and left the M&M's. Niall had even dressed up for the occasion. He had a gross plastic mask from Spirit, the Halloween specialty store that only opened for the month of October, and he used it as protection between the sand and the ass of his jeans.

"You know where we're going?" I asked Poppy.

"Give me some credit," she said. "I've lived here my entire life."

"Yeah, but you're, like, twelve, Pops."

"You're so weird," Poppy said. "I bet you weren't even popular at your old school."

"I was okay," I said, caught off-guard by her bitchy comment.

Poppy led the way through the river bottom. The grass was up to my thighs and we mostly kept to the paved paths. I could hear the Old Man River rushing by us on the right. I hugged my arms around my chest and stayed five steps back. Poppy looked like the skinniest Himalayan guide, her purple parka leading us to safety.

"You high again today, Hunter?" Poppy asked me.

"No."

"Sure," Poppy said.

Poppy walked her requisite five steps in front of me. I had memorized the back of her head, her high ponytail swinging. It bugged me a bit that she thought I was a pothead. I hadn't been back to the house downtown since I took Poppy. Who would have guessed she'd be familiar with half the people there.

"Hey, Hunter?" Poppy asked, calling back to me.

"What?"

"There's somewhere I have to go tomorrow afternoon. Want to come with me?"

Sometimes Poppy was the biggest little enigma I knew.

"Somewhere?" I said. "Want to be more specific?"

"Just tell me yes or no," she said.

"Sure," I said quickly, not wanting her to give up on me. "I'll go with you."

Me and Poppy went down to the river and sat on the cool flat rocks. She skipped a couple into the water. When it was time to go back, Poppy purposefully took the long way to the fort, avoiding the bridge completely. I didn't know how she could ignore it like that. All I wanted to do was tip my head back and look up through the metal trestles. But Poppy avoided it.

We were late to meet her mom and to get a ride back home. Poppy didn't say a word as she climbed into the front seat of the car. She just blasted the music again and went back to ignoring me.

The next day, me and Poppy left her house after lunch, when her mom had to run some errands. She led the way, with me just a step or two behind her. I counted each step I took.

Mom was big into pedometers for a while. She read somewhere that a healthy human being is supposed to take 10,000 steps a day. I can't remember how close to that she actually got. The pedometer didn't really measure how much she moved around in the yoga classes she taught. Seeing a big 2,500, day after day, got to be depressing for a health nut like Mom.

I was already at six hundred steps when Poppy turned

up a street I'd never been to before. I didn't ask questions. Maybe I was going to get my 10,000 in. Then I'd have something to tell Mom when I called home. A conversation starter that was better than announcing that my blood work was normal week after week.

The counting was drawing attention to something else I'd been doing lately. Numbering the days since Niall went under. Three hundred and twenty-seven.

I thought about Niall at night, right before I slipped away into sleep. That's when I wondered how it was for him. What it looked like on the other side. A deep black hole that he could finally slide down. Jump down. Leap into.

I took another step after Poppy.

Nine hundred.

"So, we're going to real school now?" I called up to Poppy. She'd turned up the long sidewalk that led into the high school.

She shrugged her shoulders and I watched them rise and fall from behind. I imagined she was a gopher. Just poking out of her hole to take a look around. Shrugging herself back down again.

We walked into the school. It'd been so long since I'd been inside one. The long, waxed hallways with broken-up and busted lockers lining the sides. You could see shoulder marks dug into the metal, from where someone got pissy and slammed a poor kid into his locker.

I think I figured this was the last place Poppy would want to be. There was no way I could've guessed she'd barge right in through the front doors.

"Jesus, Pops, can you slow down? What are we doing here?"

Poppy spun around on her heels and waited for me to catch up. She could've fit in here. She had an army-green jacket on today, something fitted with a hood and buttoned cuffs. It was cooler than what she normally wore. She had tight jeans with brown ankle boots. Drop her into any school and she'd at least be middle-tier, if not floating with the popular kids. Maybe a popular kid who opted into band.

Scratch that.

Opted into choir. That was cooler.

"Someone stole something from my house," Poppy said. "I'm getting it back. Are you coming?"

"Christ," I said. "What'd they steal?"

She'd already hurried ahead of me. I couldn't tell what her final destination was. Even though a high school is a high school is a high school, it's still hard to pinpoint just where exactly the littlest-Poppy-who-could was heading. Cafeteria? The office? Library?

I heard the cheering before I saw the open double doors. Poppy was making a beeline right for them.

The gym.

"Poppy!" I yelled. She disappeared through the opening without taking a second look in my direction.

The school floor was so shiny I swore I could almost see my own distorted reflection in it. Chasing after a pre-teen. Keeping her out of trouble. It shouldn't have been so hard to walk through a pair of double doors, but it was giving me some major anxiety. I took a little breath, feeling like the opposite of a man, and followed Poppy in.

I couldn't find her right away. The bleachers were just a wall of indistinguishable faces. I couldn't tell one from another. The sound in the gym was as blurry as the crowd. Just a wall of noise, all of it cheering, aimed at the center of the court.

I looked at the court just in time to get hit in the face with a flying basketball. It knocked against my cheek like a fist, making my entire face vibrate. The basketball bounced away and to the door, where an old man picked it up and threw it back to center. The cheering switched right over to laughter. Me, the butt of the joke in a school I didn't even go to. I lifted my hand in a wave—an *I'm okay* gesture that everyone ignored. Poppy didn't step forward to claim me. I leaned up against the wall, taking a breather before venturing further in to find her.

"Hunter, dude. That really you?"

Now I was sure I was hallucinating from the hit I took to my face. The basketball knocking loose some brain matter and making me confused. Because I could swear that Josh was standing in front of me, lanky as ever, wearing a red basketball jersey with matching shorts.

"Josh?"

"Shit, man. What are you doing in Alberta?"

"What are you doing in Alberta?"

Josh barked out a laugh and leaned over. He put his elbows on his thighs and caught a breath.

"Playing basketball. We got a tournament. This is where you're living now? Middle of nowhere?"

"It's a city," I told him.

"Guess we're not here long enough to see any of it," Josh said.

"When are you leaving?"

"Tonight. Heading up to Calgary next. Coach set this all up. Giving us a little tour of the prairies. We've been riding around in a charter bus for the last week. We're heading back to Victoria in a couple of days."

"Man, I wish I'd known."

"I asked your parents about you a couple of times. They wouldn't tell me where you were living. I never would've guessed here, that's for sure. So they did a good job hiding you where no one would look."

A whistle blew a shrieking pitch and Josh looked toward center court.

"I better go. Are you sticking around?" he asked.

"I don't know. I'm looking for someone."

Josh raised an eyebrow. "What kind of someone?"

"It's a long story," I told him. I got in a bit closer, a shuffle step toward him. "You heard anything about Niall?" I asked him.

Josh's face pinched up. He shook his head slow. Looked like a scene from a Zack Synder movie. Everything made more serious by drawing it out.

"He hasn't changed, man," Josh said. "Sorry."

Josh gave me a slap on the back before joining the rest of his team. I recognized them in the weird way you know people from school. I didn't hang out with any of them but we'd had classes together. Maybe it was because Alberta was the last place any of them expected me to be, but no one took a second look over.

I scanned the bleachers again, wanting to find Poppy and get out of there. As good as it was to see Josh, it also brought up a heap of things I had successfully pushed out of the way when I moved in with Aunt Lynne. As good as it was to see him, nothing had changed. Nothing made any of it even a little bit better.

Poppy materialized to my left, shooting me a look from hell. "Okay, let's go."

"You get what you came for?" I asked her.

She was wearing a backpack over her shoulder. She pulled it tighter.

"Yeah."

She led the way out of the gym, but I wasn't letting her get away with her five-steps-ahead rule. I wanted to know what was so important that she had to go in there for it.

I waited until we were outside the school and out on the front lawn before I grabbed the hanging strap of the backpack. That was the problem with the one-strap operation. Made it easy for someone like me to pull a trick like that and tug the whole thing off. Poppy stopped in her tracks.

"Let go," she said, her voice firm.

"Who'd you get this from? You disappeared, Pops. If you're going to drag me out of the house on some mission, you better tell me what it is."

"It's nothing," she said.

Maybe I was just a bully, because I yanked hard on

the backpack strap right then and pulled the entire thing away from her body. It was lighter than I thought it would be. Even though I didn't know what was in there, I guess I figured there would be some weight to it.

"Give it back."

I was already unzipping the zipper. I had a good foot in height on Poppy. I kept the pack above her head, doing everything just out of her reach.

"No, I want to know what was so important that I had to run into Josh," I said. "That was my high school basketball team in there. Not that you noticed. I moved here to get away from people I used to know. You dragged me right into it."

That got her to stop. It gave me a chance to look into the backpack and figure out what was so important. But it was nothing. Just an old pair of brown boots. Men's boots.

Poppy didn't explain. She slung the pack over her shoulder and walked home.

On the Bus

"How old is she again?" Lee asked. We were careening around a mountain corner on our way to Kelowna. I was sitting beside her, leaving Poppy snoozing by the window.

"Twelve."

We were both looking at Poppy. She had been sleeping for almost half an hour. I'd watched her head bob forward about a million times before she let it drop on the headrest behind her.

"And what? You're at her house every day?"

"Homeschool," I told her. My hand formed a semi-cool finger-gun and I pretended to shoot it into the seat ahead of me. "Pretty cool, huh?"

"So they didn't send you to school?"

"Yeah, because that was working so well before."

The bus ride was filled with more of these awkward quiet moments than the catching-up you'd think we'd be doing. Both of us working hard at considering our response, steering into the right direction.

"What was that like?" she finally asked.

"She's a cool kid. Kind of quiet. We just hung out and did work."

I thought about us sitting at the big wooden table in the kitchen, with Poppy and her eyebrows focused on her paper. She'd give me this look all the time, when I was playing around or not doing work, this one that stopped me right in my tracks.

"And so, what? No drugs? Nothing? Just living with your aunt and hanging out with her?" She bobbed her head in Poppy's direction.

"Jesus, Lee," I said. Holy hell all up in my cheeks. Instant red.

"Okay, okay," she said. "Just asking. Because before you left," Lee started.

"I know. I'm not doing anything,"

I was only lying halfway. A white lie. Barely a lie at all.

We stopped in Vernon to let a handful of people off the bus. The driver stretched his legs outside, loading and unloading luggage from the storage underneath. I watched him out the window. He had a Santa Claus beard, white at the top, but still grey at the bottom. The hipster couple with the laptop got off the bus together. The girl pulled her toque down over her hair, messing up her bangs.

It was a knee-jerk response, I guess, that made me reach over and tuck Lee's hair behind her ear. Her long bangs escaped from her ponytail. She blinked her eyes closed, her long eyelashes brushing against her cheeks. I put my thumb on there, on her closed eyelid, gentle as possible. She pushed her cheek into my palm. My hand shaped like a c, holding the side of her face.

"Can we not fight about Poppy?" I asked. "She's cool, Lee. And she's been through some stuff. And we're not going to talk about it right now. That's her thing, and she hasn't even talked about it to me."

"What do you mean?"

"Nothing," I said. "Can we not talk about Poppy?"

Lee nodded against my hand.

"We can not talk about Poppy."

Across the aisle, Poppy looked like she was still asleep. But I knew it was completely possible that she was pretending, and she'd listened to the whole thing. Lee opened her eyes again. She made an easy smile.

"Have you seen him?" I asked Lee.

She shook her head slowly.

"No."

"Who has?"

"Josh, I think. Some people went from school. A big group. His parents are there."

The bus started to go into a long dark tunnel leading through the mountain. The driver honked three times, the sound echoing off the walls. I made a wish because I was supposed to. Closed my eyes and hoped.

It was Aunt Lynne's idea for me to go swimming. I shit you not, she thought it was a good idea for me to get back in the water.

Swimming was just one more activity tacked on to the end of a long list of activities. Aunt Lynne shuffled me from appointment to appointment, from lesson to lesson. I had almost zero downtime and, any time I had a spare minute to myself, I ended up using it up on Poppy.

Aunt Lynne bought me a pair of trunks at SportChek before she took me to the pool. She didn't check my size or ask for my preference of color. So I ended up with a pair of black large. Could've mistaken me for a killer whale.

Instead of dropping me off at the pool, Aunt Lynne found a parking space in the lot and came in with me.

"Don't you have errands to run or something?" I asked her.

She patted her purse. "I brought a magazine. I'll wait until you're done."

Aunt Lynne went up to the observation deck, the poolside edition of something out of *Star Trek*, to keep an eye on me from overhead. This pool was bigger than the community pool I'd taken swimming lessons at in Victoria. A pair of diving boards were at one end and a pale blue shallow area at the other. The middle pool was divided into ten skinny lanes. Six of them were marked by upright flutter boards. Free-swim lanes.

"You sure you're serious?" I yelled up at Aunt Lynne.

She didn't look away from her magazine. Kim Kardashian's big lips were staring me right in the face from the back of us Weekly, but Aunt Lynne wasn't giving me the time of day. I adjusted my backpack over my shoulder and went back to the change rooms to switch over into my trunks. I took my time about it. No reason to rush things. Chlorinated water would have no problem going up my nose any time of the day.

While I changed, I thought about something Poppy had said the other day. She asked me a question about the ocean as we were working on Science short answers at her kitchen table. We were doing tides. In and out, ebb and flow.

Did you ever just go swim in the ocean? she asked me. Like, just run out on the beach and jump in and go for a swim?

It took me off guard. Lots of Poppy's questions weren't the ones I was ever expecting. They were just to the side of normal. Or else they started out okay and then they took a weird turn.

Stop, I wanted to tell her. Don't ask about that.

She didn't know what happened out on the ocean with Niall that day—that I really had jumped into the ocean and swam for my life. It wasn't her fault she didn't know. But at that moment, I wanted her to be smart enough to just guess the right answer. I wanted her to be a mind reader, and to turn that power on to find out about Niall, and then I wanted her to turn it right off again, just as fast.

After I'd pulled on my trunks, I went out and found an empty free-swim lane. Aunt Lynne was pretending that she couldn't see me over the top of her magazine. She was looking, though. Her eyes flittered all around, making sure they never let me out of their sight.

I put my arms up over my head. My shoulders were stiff. It was the first time I would be going under since going out on the ocean with Niall. The water was sloshing lazily up and over the lip of the pool. I tested it out with my toes. Warm as stepping into a bath. But when I jumped in and all the water rushed over my head, it was ice cold.

My chest went tight. I held on to the last breath that I'd taken and refused to let it go. The feeling of the water wasn't the same, swimming in a pool. Even though I was letting myself sink down to the bottom, there was still a bottom, and I could see it clearly even without goggles. I could make out the four easy borders of the pool, the walls that were keeping me inside.

It was a different feeling, swimming in the ocean. That's what I would have told Poppy the other day, if I had been able to make up a sentence on the spot. If I had been ready for her question. Because when I jumped into the ocean that day with Niall, there were no boundaries. I could've chosen to swim a mile in any direction, and I still wouldn't have hit a border. There was no way to tell when an end was going to come.

The chlorine was starting to burn my eyes, but I made myself stay down for another full minute. One slow count to sixty.

I finally launched myself off the bottom of the pool and exploded out of the water. The ledge of the pool was close enough to touch. I hadn't even gone that far out. I anchored myself to the side of the pool and waited to catch my breath.

Up on the observation deck, Aunt Lynne had dropped her magazine. She was on her feet, stick straight, looking right at me. The look on her face. I'd never even seen my parents wear a look like that. I'd disappeared under the water for longer than I was supposed to.

I lifted my hand in a wave to let her know I was okay. That Queen Elizabeth II that I used to exchange with Bridget on a daily basis. Just a quick turn of the hand, the way the Queen did it from her car to acknowledge the peasants.

Aunt Lynne lifted her right hand to her temple and gave me a quick salute. It was the most unexpected thing. Like she was recognizing my decision to come back up to the surface. Respecting that it had been a choice to do it. She returned to her magazine. This time she didn't flit her eyes over the top again. This time she trusted me.

I breathed in another quick breath and then went straight into a front crawl. I'd forgotten what it felt like to swim for fun. Arms and legs going at the same time, but working on opposite tasks. One kicking, one pulling at the water. It was like the patting-your-head-and-rubbing-your-stomach thing, but way more natural than that. My limbs just knew what to do, which meant I could zone out. My body moving independently of me, taking me from one end of the pool and back again.

It was real exercise. I'd been going on walks with Poppy, but walking like that wasn't a workout. It didn't make me sweat or breathe heavy. Swimming hard was real exercise. I was gasping for my breath after twenty laps.

I flipped over and started on my back crawl, using the lane dividers to keep me guided in the right direction.

I lost myself in that swimming. I did it for another hour, only vacating the lane when the pool was closing.

Aunt Lynne's piano students had been practicing Christmas carols since the end of November. It was every combination of those classics that you could think up: "Frosty the Snowman." "Jingle Bells." "Silent Night." "All I Want for Christmas Is You." A whole house full of them on repeat, the only difference between them the quality. I was sick of them all by the start of December. Heard them all about fifty times each.

Even writing out Math equations in semi-silence was better than sitting at Aunt Lynne's house with eardrums bleeding Christmas music.

"How many do you have left?" Poppy asked me, the second week of December, near the end of our semester.

I counted them up in my book. Calculus was the worst. I had completed maybe two full equations in an hour.

"Uh, like, all of them," I said.

Poppy shut my Math book, slamming down the front cover.

"Want to go to the mall?" she said.

"Not really."

"Mom wants us to go."

"And do what?"

Poppy pulled two twenty-dollar bills out of the pocket of her jeans.

"Spend this," she said. "It's like an end-of-the-semester present."

"You're serious?" I asked her. "We're not going to leave the house and spend your mom's money and then get back here and have her be all pissed?"

Poppy pocketed the money and pushed away from the table.

"Come on," she said. "I don't want to be the only person on the bus."

One of the first things I'd really noticed about Lethbridge was that the bus service was seriously crappy and underused. Pretty often, you'd look through the window of a bus heading downtown and see it empty, except for the bus driver. It was the saddest when there was just a single passenger sitting mid-bus. Staring out the window. Looking lonely. So I knew what Poppy meant by not wanting to be alone. And twenty bucks was twenty bucks.

We walked to the end of the street and waited for the first bus to come by. I didn't want to walk through the snow to the mall. I'd never got around to getting a pair of boots and the powder stuck to my shoes and got into my socks. Poppy was bundled up for the weather. Complete with pom-pom hat.

The mall was a depressing place. People sat out on the front steps, smoking and looking sketchy. Poppy walked right past them, holding the door open for me like I was her kid. She switched roles on me, making me out to be the younger, less experienced one.

"You want to split up or something?" I asked her.

She was examining the mall, her eyes flitting to the corners. I'd seen her do it before. In public places, she always surveyed the space first. She finally gave me a shrug and we stuck together.

I bought us two smoothies from Orange Julius and we had a Cinnabon, too. It was a good thing I was swimming again. Aunt Lynne had taken me three more times. I was feeling less like the sack of potatoes I was becoming back at home.

Christmas season meant the mall was packed. It was hard to find a table in the food court and we ended up finishing our smoothies on a bench in front of the movie theaters. And, surprise, the Christmas music was streaming through the entire mall, following me everywhere.

"What do you do for Christmas at home?" Poppy asked me.

Sometimes I thought she was playing a game with me or asking me a random thing just to fill up the silence. But this time she seemed genuinely interested. Her straw was poking up out of her smoothie cup and resting on her lower lip.

"Not too much," I told her. "We usually open a present each on Christmas Eve, and it's almost always pajamas or a movie that we all watch together. Me, my parents, and Bridge. We make a big breakfast on Christmas morning. That's about it. Probably this year it's not going to be much of anything. My sister's spending Christmas in Australia. It doesn't make sense for her to zip home for the holiday. And it looks like I'll be spending Christmas here."

"You're not going home?"

"I don't think so," I said. But, really, I wasn't sure. Christmas had never come up in my phone calls home. Mom and Dad liked to keep it in the immediate present. Not too far forward and definitely never backward. But I realized I'd be fine if it was just me and Aunt Lynne. That didn't sound bad at all.

"What about you?" I said, turning it back to her.

Poppy bounced the straw between her teeth. There were tiny chew marks all over the place. I used to hate it when Bridge did that to the straw of the drink we'd share at a movie. She'd chomp it all up like a piece of gum until it was too gross to use. Poppy bit down again.

"Nothing," she finally answered. "Christmas sucks at my house."

She tossed the rest of her Orange Julius in the trash and headed down the mall.

"You gotta stop doing that," I said, catching up with her.

"What? You wanted to sit on the bench all day?"

"No," I said, matching her pace. "Just don't jet off. I don't magically know where you're going."

She stopped where she was. She was so much shorter than me, which made her seem even more like a little kid.

"Fine," she said. "Lead the way."

"Look," I said. "If something's wrong, tell me, okay? I can't guess."

"Nothing's wrong," Poppy said.

Something was. The look on her face was killer.

"Let's go spend your mom's money," I told her.

We walked through the mall with our arms touching. I didn't even mind the Christmas music.

"Hunter!"

Aunt Lynne was calling downstairs, trying to get my attention. I put my head around the doorway to yell back up at her.

"Give me a sec," I said. "I'm just on the phone with Bridge."

"Play through," Aunt Lynne said, as if we were on a golf course. Ducking those round white golf balls. Dodging a dodgy swing from a club.

Whatever Aunt Lynne needed me for, it was going to have to wait. The doorbell rang through the house, signaling the arrival of another piano student. One more week and Aunt Lynne would be on her holiday hiatus until the New Year. Until then, it was lessons every afternoon after school got out until nine o'clock at night. Aunt Lynne always missed the best shows on cable. I had to Tivo them for her to watch right before she went to bed.

"So, like I was saying," I continued telling Bridget on the phone, "Mom and Dad haven't said anything about Christmas. So I'm pretty sure it's going to be just me and Aunt Lynne. Maybe we'll all conference call you into Christmas morning. It could be a real party."

"Do not do that," she said. "I don't want to be depressed on Christmas."

"Your loss."

Bridget snorted. She sounded far away when she spoke, not a bad connection but a weak one. She was using an outdated pay-as-you-go phone. It didn't even have the Internet. She couldn't send pictures through text message.

"So you're done homeschooling for the semester?" You could hear the derision in her voice. Making total fun of the fact that I was a homeschooled student.

"Yeah," I said. "Guess so."

"When do you know if you're staying for the whole year? I mean, shouldn't you figure that out? If you have to get back home and register for the second semester of school, or if you're just going to keep doing what you're doing in Alberta?"

"Bridge," I said. "I'm in the dark on this. Complete black-out on information."

"I'll see what I can find out," she said. "I'm calling Mom and Dad next."

"Let me know."

"Is that girl next door still bugging you?" Bridget asked.

"Poppy," I said. "And it's 'girl across the alley.' Her backyard's right behind Aunt Lynne's house. And, yeah, I see her mostly every day."

The first time I talked to Bridget on the phone, I had led in with the fact that Poppy was a little strange. I think I said a couple of not choice words about her that I couldn't take back. They'd colored Bridget's entire perception of her.

"Be careful, okay?" Bridget said. "She sounds a little strange."

"I know. But she's all right."

We left a silence over the phone. I don't think I've ever heard a silence that I didn't want to immediately fill up. Except for with Niall. Those were easy silences. And maybe Poppy had the potential to leave some good ones, too.

"I better go," Bridget said. "I don't want to use up all of my credit on you."

"Don't get sunburnt," I told her.

"SPF 50," she signed off.

Upstairs, a student was banging out a clumsy "Joy to the World." I waited for him to finish before I knocked on the wall of the piano room. Aunt Lynne swiveled her head like an owl.

"Did you need something?" I asked her.

"Poppy called. You should go over there if you're not doing anything."

Poppy was at the front of her house, shoveling the driveway. The schhh schhh of the plastic on snowy cement was the winter equivalent of that droning sound that plays in the background of televised golf. Background noise that sounds exactly like the season.

"Hey, Pops," I said. "My aunt said you called."

"Mom asked me to shovel the driveway and the sidewalk before dinner," Poppy said. "Want to help?"

Poppy hadn't made more than a dent in the shoveling. There had been a fresh dump of snow the night before.

"You got an extra shovel?"

"In the garage," Poppy said.

I found the shovel, purple plastic at the end of a long wooden handle. I almost wanted to borrow a pair of snow boots at the same time, from where they were all lined up on a boot rack. The mysterious boots from Poppy's backpack were there, too. They seemed like the least likely item to be stolen out of Poppy's garage. Questions were pretty one-way with that kid. I didn't think I'd get another chance to ask about the boots. Not without her getting mad at me. Storming away.

I left my questions in the garage and walked out with the shovel. Between the swimming and the shoveling, I was getting kind of ripped. Friends in BC would hardly recognize me.

Poppy took care of the sidewalks while I did most of the driveway. Maybe monotonous workouts were the ones for me. Lifting. Shoveling. Swimming. Zoning-out activities.

I tried to figure out what the time spent shoveling here was allocated to in Victoria, where shoveling almost never happened. Probably in raking up the leaves in the fall. They crunched underfoot from October until November. Crunched before they turned soggy from the rain.

"Mind if I get some water?" I asked Poppy. I was sweating under my winter coat. Dress to impress for the weather and you ended up sweating right out of your clothes.

"Bring me one, too," she said. "Actually, I think I want a Coke."

"You got it," I said.

I knew Poppy's house just about as well as Aunt Lynne's. Spending almost every day over there made it back-of-the-hand knowledge. I went into the kitchen and poured a glass of water from the sink. The Coke was in the fridge. I grabbed a can for Poppy.

Normally the kitchen table was completely clear, except for when me and Poppy were doing our homework. But today there was a big cardboard box sitting right in the center. The flaps were open. It was out of place in the tiny kitchen. Old newspaper articles were folded at the top. The pages weren't yellowed—they weren't that old—but they weren't the off-white of day-of-publication.

A picture and a headline on the top article were clearly visible. A light crease through the middle. It was easy enough to flatten it out against the table.

Brent Haynes. There was a photo of him with the article, a grainy black and white. Poppy was almost a spitting image of him. Same nose, eyes, and expression. So this was Poppy's dad. He was wearing a sharp suit and carrying a briefcase. Snapped leaving a building downtown. The headline said the guy had stolen millions.

"Jesus."

I reached for another article. This one gave more background information on Poppy's dad. He worked at an investment firm. He started taking more than he invested.

A whole lot more.

"What are you doing?"

Poppy was in the kitchen. She had a look on her face that almost matched her dad's expression in the newspaper picture. Sad and tired and sorry.

"Getting your Coke," I told her.

The look on her face was breaking my heart.

"Get away from that," she said. "It's not supposed to be down here."

"Was your mom going through it?"

"My mom is always going through it," she said quietly.

She took the article from my hand. Even though I could tell she was mad, she took it so gently. As if not to rip it.

"Is that why your dad's gone?" I asked her. "Because he stole some money?"

Poppy put the folded article back in the box. She shut the flaps and overlapped them, sealing the contents inside.

"Yeah," she said, monotone. "That's why he's gone."

Poppy wouldn't look at me. She took the box upstairs and didn't come down again.

Finally, I went back to Aunt Lynne's house. Heat was creeping through my chest and up my face. You know when someone quiet talks in class, and that area where their necklace hangs flushes this horrible red? You feel more embarrassed for them than you ever have before. I had that in an all-over-body sensation.

"Did you help?" Aunt Lynne asked.

It took me a minute to understand. The whole reason for going over to Poppy's was to shovel that goddamn sidewalk.

Not mess everything up between us.

"Guess so," I said.

"Well, you can do ours next. The city slaps you with a fine if the walks aren't done."

"You've been here all morning," I said.

"I didn't have time. Besides," she tousled my hair, a weird, little-kid gesture, "that's what I've got a tenant for. The shovel's in the garage. Do that and I'll bring a pizza home for dinner."

She shrugged on her jacket. A purple pea coat. Her boots clip-clopped across the floor.

Aunt Lynne's car started up in the driveway. She had been darting out to elementary schools since the start of December. She was playing piano for the Christmas concerts. When she talked about visiting the schools, it made me kind of miss it. All that tinsel, and candy canes passed out in the bleachers. I almost wanted to tag along with her.

She'd said, 'I'll bring pizza.' That meant an ETA of around dinnertime. The afternoon stretched out long and tunnel-like.

Shoveling was going to be hard with those tire tracks across the snow. I wouldn't be able to get it down to the pavement. I drained a can of Coke from the fridge. Supplies in the cupboard were low. I found a box of Chewy granola bars, the ones with a big peanut crossed out in red, nut-free for the allergic types. I ate a couple of them. MTV was counting down the top hundred songs of the 90s in anticipation of New Year's. Man, I was glad I didn't grow up in that decade. All that plaid and loose, light jeans. Tom Cochrane came on singing "Life is a Highway" and, I swear to God, I'd never have guessed he looked like that in about a million years. Floppy blond hair and baggy clothing. Plus, you never see dudes wearing wedding rings in music videos anymore. They don't want to advertise that shit.

I went back for the last granola bar. Saw this flash of purple out the window. Poppy was undoing her back gate. Stepping through. Shutting it behind her. She walked fast, knowing exactly where she was going. My grandma used to have a dog like that. A German Shepherd who walked so purposefully, it bulldozed everything to get to where it was going. Poppy had that German Shepherd way of walking.

I swallowed my granola bar down with the rest of the Coke. I tried to get my purposeful walk on. Maybe not so much German Shepherd as Golden Retriever. Loping along. I shadowed Poppy—my version of a spy movie—while she trotted up the road.

I could almost pretend we were going on one of our normal everyday walks. She was always a good couple of feet ahead of me. Taking the role of the dickish fast-walking boyfriend who leaves his girl, tottering in high heels, behind.

At first I thought she was going to the high school again. She started off in that direction but, instead of turning up the sidewalk, she kept right on walking. Speed-walking. There's an Olympic sport for that. It's the most hilarious thing to watch on TV. But I swear, Poppy would kill at that event.

When we had been walking for fifteen minutes, no sign of

stopping, I stuffed my ear buds in and listened to the music on my phone. It was some techno, a good beat with a sound like lasers over top. I turned it up to almost-max. The sound of it drove my feet forward. Keeping Poppy's pace, just a good twenty feet behind her.

It took me a while to clue in to where we were going. Don't get me wrong—I knew my way around Lethbridge. Three months was enough time to explore almost all of that tiny city. From the Costco end to the University. But Poppy was taking us back to somewhere we'd already been before. Or almost-been.

The Galt Museum in Lethbridge was pretty old. Aunt Lynne told me it used to be a hospital before they turned it into a museum, meaning everyone had a ghost story to tell about it. Kids staring out of upstairs windows. Clanking sounds in the basement. Unexplained visitors who were never really there at all. It was all bullshit. But Aunt Lynne liked to share her stories, grinning wildly as she explained the unexplained.

The building was right on the edge of the coulees, which seemed risky to me. I never knew what a coulee was before I moved to Alberta. Turns out they're these rolling hills, only nowhere near as sturdy. They were falling in all the time all over the city, and the people who built their houses on them had to watch them slide. Tumble down. The museum was way out there. It had a nice view, in line with the high-level bridge above the river.

Poppy didn't go into the museum. Instead, she walked around to the back, taking the tiny snow-covered red-ash path out where it twisted across the open coulee. Two people were out there already. Skinny jeans and hoodies. The two girls from the dealer's house. Poppy went straight toward them, not beating around the bush. But it was all open on the coulee. If I went any further forward on the curved path, Poppy would see me, catching me head on.

I had to lurk back by the museum. Squinted my eyes. Poppy had bounded right up to the two girls but, now that she was close, she was acting differently. If she had a shell like a turtle's, it would be up by her shoulders. She would be halfway to creeping back inside of her house.

It was hard to tell if Poppy had a plan. If she did, then it was going wrong. The girls were closing in on her, a v-shaped attack. The brown-haired girl grabbed the sleeve of Poppy's coat. She yanked hard, pulling Poppy toward her. The other girl, a Starbucks Blonde Roast, must've been waiting for Poppy to get that close. She slapped her, an open-palmed hit.

"Hey, hey, hey," I yelled, cover blown. I made a beeline for the girls and stepped between them and Poppy.

Poppy lashed out, her tiny fists flying. She popped the blonde girl in the face, making her nose spray red. Poppy took a blow of her own, as high as her eyebrow.

The two girls were collecting themselves, breathing hard and getting ready to come after Poppy again. Again I got between them and Poppy. "You two get out of here. Fuck off and leave her alone."

"Hunter," Poppy said. "Get off."

She shrugged away from me and went at the two girls again.

I almost pulled her back, until I realized she wasn't trying to attack them. She was reaching for a canvas bag hanging over the brown-haired girl's shoulder. Poppy pulled it hard.

"Ow." The girl rubbed at her shoulder.

Once Poppy had the bag, she took off in the direction she'd come from.

"Hey," I yelled. "Hey!"

I caught her up in the museum parking lot. Grabbed her by the arm and made her turn around and look at me.

"Shit," I said. Maybe she gave that one chick a bloody nose, but she had a cut through her left eyebrow.

"Yeah, she got me. Big deal."

"Big deal," I mimicked. "What the hell happened? What was that about?"

"Nothing," she mumbled. Then she turned to steel. "What were you doing following me? You creep."

"Don't make this about me." While she wasn't ready for it, I grabbed her canvas bag. Yanked it off her shoulder hard. "What's even in this? What'd you go back for?"

It wasn't a pair of boots this time, but it wasn't anything much better. Nothing that seemed worth getting in a fight over. Just an old leather jacket. Worn and creased.

Something clicked. A snap into place.

"It's your dad's, hey?" I said. Toned my voice right down. I felt it scratch from when I'd yelled at the girls to leave her alone. "Why'd they have it?"

Poppy shrugged, lips zipped.

"Don't do that," I said. "Just give me an answer."

She took off ahead of me. Back to ten paces in front and me ten paces behind. I let her walk home like that. All the way back, a thirty-minute hike. When we turned down our street, I finally stopped her with my hand on her shoulder.

"Come over to Aunt Lynne's," I said. "You should clean that. If it gets infected, you could lose your whole eye or something."

Poppy followed me into the house, where I went to the bathroom and got some stuff together from the medicine cupboard. It was funny to sit Poppy down at the table and fix her up. I swabbed some antiseptic cream on a Kleenex and dabbed it all over her eyebrow. I cleaned it off and did the same thing all over again, this time with Polysporin.

"How big does a cut have to be to get stitches?" she asked me.

"Beats me."

She put her hand to her eyebrow. "It doesn't feel that bad."

"Think a Band-aid will do?"

"Yeah."

I stuck it on. Perched above her eye, the Band-aid turned her into a pirate.

"You're right," Poppy said, finally answering my question. "The jacket's my dad's. So were the boots. The ones I got back from the high school."

"I figured," I said. "What were those girls doing with it?"

"It's kind of a game." Poppy fiddled with her Band-aid, pressing at it with the heel of her hand. "To steal stuff that belonged to my dad."

"From your house?"

"Yeah," she said.

"Dude, that's police business. You should call them."

"Mom has. They stop for a while and then they try again. They steal something from us since he stole so much from them."

"That's fucked up."

Poppy shrugged her shoulders, avoiding eye contact.

"Poppy," I started. "Should we talk about that? About what was in that box."

"I don't want to," she said, quietly. "I really don't."

The doorbell rang, clanging through the house. I ignored it. It was the worst time to leave Poppy by herself. But the doorbell was followed by a hard knock, a repeating pattern.

"I'll be right back," I told her. "Hang on."

When I opened the front door of Aunt Lynne's house, Lee was standing there on the front step. Her cheeks were rosy red from the cold. She waved a gloved hand at me, even though I was a foot away from her.

"Hey," she said. And then, smiling, "Fancy meeting you here."

There were only a handful of reasons for Lee to be here. None of them were good.

"What happened?"

Lee shifted from foot to foot.

"It's Niall."

"Is he okay?"

"You have to come home," she said.

My legs went to Jell-O, making it hard to stay standing. I pressed my shoulder up against the wall, trying to find a way to answer.

"I can't."

"I came up here on the Greyhound. I have a return ticket for tomorrow. I booked you one, too. First thing in the morning."

"Jesus. You're serious."

"Hunter?" Next to Lee, Poppy looked like a ten-year-old. Maybe I'd gotten used to the way Poppy sometimes seemed older than she was but, next to Lee, she looked just like a kid again. And I could see her noticing it. The way I saw her.

"Hey," Lee said, sticking out her hand, "I'm Lee. I'm a friend of Hunter's."

"From Victoria," Poppy said, stating the fact.

"Yeah," she said.

"So, what, you're going home?" Poppy asked me.

She said it straight and easy. I wanted to think she didn't care. But she did, more than I'd thought. I went into the kitchen, Poppy following close behind me. Part of me didn't want Lee to hear all of this.

"I guess I'm going tomorrow," I said. "Lee came to get me. We have a friend. Niall. I have to go back because of him."

"You're seriously leaving," Poppy said.

"I have to," I said.

Poppy's fingers started tapping on the doorframe. "Good," she said. "I wanted to see where you live."

I carefully shook my head. "You can't come."

"'Course I can," Poppy said. Her hands reached up

behind her head to tighten her ponytail. It raised up an inch in height, gave her a peacock flair.

"You can't," I said. "There's no way."

Poppy took a step forward.

"You have to take me," she said.

Poppy's forehead Band-aid was small and ugly. The flesh color stood out against her face. Her expression was set in stone. A gargoyle face.

"You're serious," I said.

"Take me with you," she said again.

"Poppy, Victoria's a long way."

"Yeah," she said. "And we'll come back here when you're done doing whatever you have to do."

But whatever it was with Niall, who knew how long it would take? Who knew what I was going back to? "I don't know."

"Please."

I sat down heavily at the kitchen table. Her mom would kill me. Aunt Lynne would kill me.

Poppy nudged the back of my chair.

"I can't just take you with me."

"You can't leave me alone," she said. "I don't want to stay here."

"Pops."

"Please," she repeated. Her pleading was so different from her usual straight talk. I clasped my hands around my neck and looked at the floor. Like maybe there would be an answer written down there. Dear Hunter, here is what you do.

Poppy was twelve years old. I couldn't just take her to the province next door without telling anyone. But if I told someone—her mom, Aunt Lynne—there was no way she would be able to go.

She sat across from me at the table. Her bangs were too long and hanging in her eyes. Her breathing was loud, like she had a stuffed-up nose.

"I'd bring you right back, two days, max," I said. "It won't be for long."

"Okay."

"But you can't tell your mom because there's no way she'd let you come."

Lee had been listening, leaning on the doorframe.

"Hunter," she said, "she can't come. She's too young."

"She can come." I turned to Lee, trying to make her see how important it was. "It'll be fine."

It was far from fine. But I couldn't leave her behind, especially with what I'd found out. It made a little more sense, the way people looked at her and her mom when they were out. The reason she was homeschooled.

So, she was coming with us.

On the Bus

We'd have an hour and a half in Kelowna.

"Do you think we should wake Poppy up?" Lee asked. "She'll probably want to get off the bus if we do."

I put my hand on Lee's thigh, fingertips on her kneecap. I made them into a spider, floating them out and then in again. I folded them into my palm and gave her a nudge on the shoulder. "Yeah."

I scooted across the aisle into the seat beside Poppy. The drawstrings on her hoodie were uneven, one hanging way lower than the other. I thought it would be funny to pull on them, wake her up that way. I thought that for maybe two seconds before I just shook her by the shoulder. "Poppy?"

"Where are we?"

She was angling her head back, away from my face. It was the way you hide fusty just-woke-up breath from whoever you're talking to. I knew that trick, but I wasn't sure if Poppy was aware she was doing it.

"Kelowna," I told her. "Come on. We're going to see what's around."

Poppy grabbed her backpack from under the seat. Me and Lee had shoved all of our stuff under the seat in front of us. Lee left a sweater draped across our two seats and a book on Poppy's to save our places.

"You want me to carry that?" I asked her, transferring the straps to my shoulders.

"Don't lose it," she said.

The snow was falling in fat flakes that stuck to our jackets. I made a circle between my thumb and my first finger and looked through. Instant telescope. It was warp speed snow, like stars shooting past us. Lee pulled my hand down away from my face and held it tight. Her mittens were so fat. I could have been holding onto a bear paw.

The snow gave us some insulation. Maybe it was ten below out or something, but it was a comfy cold. It was dead quiet.

"So, look," Lee said, pointing behind us. A small group of people from the bus were heading into town. "We can go with them and see what's in Kelowna, or we can go for a walk outside the city."

"I vote outside the city," Poppy said. She bent her knees, making a pair of chicken wings that she stretched alternately. "I got, like, a cramp or something."

"Good call," I told her. "Walk to that hill?" I suggested. It was an easy one, maybe a beginner's run on a ski hill. The moon made the snow shine silver.

Lee held on tighter to my hand. I could almost feel her fingers clenching around mine under all that layered fabric. Mittens with a pair of gloves on underneath.

"Poppy," Lee said. She held out her other hand.

"No, thanks," Poppy said.

"Pops," I said. "We're a team."

"I'm good." She shoved her hands into her pockets.

We headed to the hill. The cold hit my teeth and froze them, and I tried not to suck in the freezing air. The snow was hard to walk through, a nice layer of powder on top and a crunching ice on the bottom. My sneakers soaked up the snow with every step. Poppy was way up ahead of us. With her hood up, she looked like a baby thug, a hooligan in training.

"She's going up the hill," Lee said.

"Guess that means we are, too."

Poppy was moving at a good pace, so me and Lee started huffing up the hill. Down below, you could see some of Kelowna, the city spread out with its lights. Maybe I needed glasses, because all the light posts gave off tiny halos of light. Shit was a little blurry and I wasn't even on anything.

"Jesus. I think I'm dying," I said. We'd finally caught up with Poppy, a good halfway up the hillside. I could see my breath coming out in tiny puffs that sat on the air in front of me. That nice feeling of insulation was gone.

Lee had to take her inhaler out of her jacket pocket and take a few puffs.

"Asthma," she explained to Poppy between wheezing. "I'll be cool in a sec."

She sat down on the side of the hill and I joined her. Lee's asthma was just one of those interesting facts about her. She'd lose her breath in the spring when shit was growing again, and I'd sit beside her and wait it out. Poppy was interested. She kept a close eye on Lee.

"How are you doing?" I asked Poppy. I was still wearing her almost child-sized backpack. The straps were tight across my shoulders. "Bet Gregory wishes he was along for the ride."

"Why? You got some cat-sized winter gear somewhere?"

I said to Lee, "There's a good investment for your dad. Tell him to get working on the cat clothes."

Lee smiled at us. She was still breathing hard enough that her back lifted up and down every time she inhaled.

We were getting close to Victoria. There were a handful of stops between Kelowna and Vancouver, before a quick ferry ride across to the island. We'd be there in the morning. I'd be seeing Niall again. My palms started sweating in my gloves.

I pushed off the edge of the hill, trying to see how slippery it was, and the answer was: pretty damn slippery. Poppy and Lee were staring down at Kelowna. I grinned, ready to shake it up a little.

"See you guys," I said and pushed hard against the snow.

"Hunter!" Lee yelled.

I picked up speed, sliding down on my ass. The bottom of my jacket had less traction than my jeans, and I had it pulled down so I was really going. The trees blurred green beside me, the same as when we were in the bus, watching it all fly by. I stopped sliding a few feet from the bottom and ran the rest of the way, flying ass over teakettle, barely balanced.

Lee and Poppy slid down after.

Poppy was looking worse for wear. Her hair was shiny from being unwashed and she had dark circles under her eyes. Maybe being so tired was part of the reason she had been so desperate to come to Victoria with me. Her dad gone and her never saying a word about him. I saw the way they treated her, that group of teens out in the alley. Outside the house downtown. On the coulees. That was some leper shit, right there. Treating her as if they needed a ten-foot buffer. Maybe I'd want to leave, too, if I was her.

Lethbridge seemed like a foreign country now, compared to the top of the hill in Kelowna.

"Come on," I said. "We still have some time. Let's exercise our legs out."

I readjusted Poppy's backpack and we walked in a line again, this time without the hand-holding. But being all tied up with Lee and running for the hill was the first time I'd felt calm all day.

It was a ten-minute walk before we hit the lake, the whole thing frozen over so hard that hockey nets had been set up at either end and it had skate marks running sideways. The ice wasn't slippery in the way the packed snow on the hill was. It was outdoor ice without a Zamboni, hard and frosted. I ran across and tried to glide, but the thin blanket of snow on top made it difficult. I could feel Poppy's backpack bobbing.

Lee came out next, grabbing my hand with her gloved fingers, our palms pressed together.

"Poppy? You coming?"

"I'm okay," she said, her tiny voice coming from the side of the lake. She was sitting on top of a snow bank, holding her arms crossed against her chest.

I ran fast across the ice, daring it to make my feet slide or crack underneath. The ice held tight.

Lee ran with me, her feet more unsure. The rubber soles slid around, no grip under there. I kept checking back on Poppy, just sitting on the bank. She was too far away for me to tell what she was looking at.

"Hey," Lee said. "Stop for a sec?"

We were a hundred meters from the shore, a quick track-and-field race back. Lee caught her breath, this time *sans* inhaler.

She put her chin on my shoulder and then her cheek. Our hips swung together. We kissed again. I wrecked it by sniffing, my nose all gross and runny from the cold. Lee put her finger under my nostrils, making a comical moustache and swooping my snot at the same time.

"Nice look for you, Hunter."

"I try," I said. I kissed her on the forehead.

"We're home in the morning," she said.

Who knew what home was? Victoria, where my parents were, or back in Lethbridge, where I'd felt for a sec like I belonged.

"Are you going to stay?" Lee asked.

I hadn't thought past seeing Niall. "I don't know."

If I wanted to stay in Victoria, would my parents let me? It had been their idea to send me to Lethbridge. I didn't know if my exile was up for renegotiation. I didn't know if I wanted it to be.

"You like it there? In Lethbridge?"

"It's different," I told her.

"Different how?"

"It's easier."

There was a whole chunk of everything still in Victoria. My parents, how close I'd been with Bridget, Lee, Josh, and then there was even still some of the good stuff with Niall. Compare that to my Aunt Lynne, Poppy, and her mom, all of that new and temporary, and one of those seemed like a world that eclipses the other.

"Where's Poppy?" Lee asked, looking across the lake.

"She's over there," I said. But when I looked again, I'd lost the color of her small jacket. She had disappeared from the shore.

My legs started to melt, going jelly from the running and the walking and the deep, deep snow. But more from the absence of Poppy, the twelve-year-old-size cutout missing from the other side of the lake.

"She's got to be on the bus," Lee said. Even though she was trying to be reassuring, there was no way to hide the panic in her voice. We ran across the ice and then dragged our feet through the thick, deep snow. My thighs were on fire.

Poppy had no reason to go back to the bus. If she was running away, then she was running away from us. From me. I felt stupid for making out with Lee in the middle of the frozen lake. Poppy standing on the sidelines. She'd said she wanted to come with us, but she didn't really know what that meant, how far it was, how long it would take, anything. But the real reason she was here was because I couldn't leave her in Lethbridge. Poppy was a piece of the only place I'd felt close to normal since what happened to Niall. If I left her behind, I left that, too.

Truth was, maybe I was closer to Poppy than I was to Lee. We'd spent a lot of time together when it counted.

The bus was parked where we'd left it. A skinny line of passengers was waiting to get back on. If Poppy wasn't there, I didn't know what we were going to do.

"You go," Lee said, using her puffer again and pushing me ahead. I butted in line, taking the steps in two leaps.

Poppy wasn't in our seats. She wasn't anywhere on the bus. I made a beeline for the washroom at the back, but it was vacant and empty. I squeezed past the other passengers. That old lady gave me a look again. I gave her one right back.

"She's not on there?" Lee said.

"No. There's some stores down the street. She might be there. I'm going to go look. I'll be right back. "

"Hunter," Lee said. "Go fast. I'll stay here in case she comes back."

I took a jog in the opposite direction of the hill. That had been the worst idea. We should've all stayed on the bus and left Poppy sleeping and me and Lee being okay.

"Poppy!"

My teeth were back to freezing again. The cold sucked all the moisture out of my lips.

I spotted her jacket. "Hey!" The back of her hood. "Poppy!"

I ran to where she was standing at a street corner. Her hair stuck to her forehead. Her scarf had come undone from where Lee had tied it earlier. She looked younger than ever. What had I done, bringing her here with us?

"Where did you go?"

Poppy shrugged her shoulders.

"Heads up," she said and tossed me my phone. It made a basketball arch in the air and I palmed it.

"Did you call your mom?" Panic.

"We should get going," she said. "The bus is leaving."

"Did you?"

She shook her head. "No. I decided not to."

When we got back on the bus, everyone was eyeballing the hell out of me. Poppy settled back in her seat. I stayed, standing awkwardly in the middle of the aisle, looking down at her.

Lee put her hand on my shoulder, urging me to sit down. I had to shake myself out of it. I gave my head an actual shake.

I slid into the seat next to Poppy. "Want to watch a movie? Lee brought her laptop."

"Sure," Poppy said.

Lee retrieved her bag from under the seat and passed it over. I set up the headphones and the sound, and was just about to press Play when Poppy asked the question.

"Are you going to stay in Victoria when we get there?"

"I haven't thought about it yet," I said, hedging badly. "We still have a while before we make it."

It wasn't an answer, not even half of one. Poppy plugged in an ear bud and stared at the screen, waiting for me to start the movie.

Halfway to Merritt, I realized I still had Poppy's pink backpack slung over my shoulders, the almost weightless bag stuffed against the back of the seat. She'd fallen asleep by the time I undid it and was looking for a sweater to put on her legs, because her jeans were still wet with snow. Instead, my hand closed around a book at the bottom of her bag. She must have thrown it in to have something to do on the bus. A picture poked out of the top, a hard crease through the corner. Keeping an eye on Poppy, hoping she wouldn't wake up, I pulled gently on the corner.

I recognized Poppy and her mom, but not the face of her dad sitting beside them. He looked different from how he'd looked in the newspaper. Less grainy. Younger. The only thing I could think was that he looked like a good guy. All of the lines on his face were the ones you get from smiling and laughing all the time.

I put the picture all the way back in the book, hoping the weight of the two covers would erase the crease. I found a sweater and draped it over Poppy's legs, and finished the movie without her.

While the closing credits rolled, I took out my phone. I hadn't even noticed her take it from me. Pickpocketing me sometime when we were stopped in Kelowna. I pressed redial.

It was a Lethbridge phone number on the screen and it wasn't Poppy's. When I knew it wasn't going to her mom,

I let it keep ringing.

When it went to voicemail, I listened close.

"You have reached J.R. Duncan Financial Firm. Please leave your message."

I ended the call before the machine could record my breathing.

Poppy's eyes were shut tight. They weren't even fluttering. She wasn't just pretending.

I tried to jigsaw it together, but it made a weird kind of sense. Poppy's dad had been at a financial firm. What did Poppy want to call that number for? The company probably hadn't had her dad's name in the message for months.

Maybe she had been looking for his voice. But it had been erased.

We passed through Merritt. Hope. Chilliwack. I didn't know why BC had such good names but it did. I bet every single person who drove through wondered what it would be like to live in Hope. Hope, hope, hope.

Across the aisle, Lee was sleeping. She had her legs tucked underneath her, a dinosaur curled inside an egg. Her head against the window.

I reached into Poppy's backpack where there was a package of Mentos that I'd bought her at the gas station in Banff. I popped one out of the top. I made it last from Abbotsford to Langley, and then it melted me to sleep.

By the time we arrived in Vancouver, we didn't have any energy to even think about leaving the Greyhound Station, but we had to get off our bus and transfer to a new one. Lee thought we should go get breakfast, eat a little something before we got to the ferry terminal, but Poppy was sitting like a dead weight, and I was chilled in my still-damp pants and jacket from when we got off the bus in Kelowna. It was so early that the sun wasn't even up yet, keeping winter hours at five-thirty this morning.

We found a row of chairs in the station. Poppy fell asleep instantly. Lee stayed to watch her while I used my phone. It was finally time to let my parents know I was coming.

The phone rang twice before Dad picked up groggily, just a brief note of panic cutting through his voice and reminding me that I was making an early morning phone call.

"Hey, Dad."

"Hunter?"

I left a little silence, picking over the words that I could choose from.

"Hey, Dad. I'm, um, almost home."

He left a neat package of quiet.

"Where are you?"

"I'm in Vancouver. Lee is here. And ..." I took Poppy out of it, just for a second. "I'm going to see Niall."

Dad didn't answer for a bit. Eventually he asked, "Are you coming to the house?"

"After."

"And then what?"

"I don't know."

Dad sighed. I heard him shift the phone from one ear to the other.

"We'll see you when you get here."

We had to get off the bus for the hour-and-a-half ferry ride. I went out to the deck, telling Lee and Poppy that I wanted to look for whales. It was bullshit. I'd taken the ferry dozens of times between Vancouver and Victoria and I'd never seen a single one. I let the icy wind blow me around out there. It was this close to being Lethbridge wind, the kind that gave you whiplash. Hurricane wind. It whipped around a couple of seagulls, giving them the eggbeater. They hung motionless in the air, even with their wings beating frantically.

We went back to the bus before the ferry docked and got ready for the final drive into the city. I took a window seat, leaving a pair of seats for Lee and Poppy to share. I recognized the terminal and the highway down to Victoria. The sun was out, rippling across the sky in a welcome home. It should be raining. It shouldn't be a sun-shiny day. It should be gray and pouring.

"Hey," Poppy said, leaning across the aisle. She pinched my arm. "This is where you're from?"

"Yeah," I said. "I lived right here on the side of the highway."

She rolled her eyes. "You know what I mean."

"Yeah," I said. "This is where I'm from."

"If I lived somewhere like this, I would never leave," Poppy said. "So why did you?"

Off the Bus

Lee had arranged for her dad to meet us at the Greyhound Station downtown. He hadn't changed. He was in his uniform of suit jacket with jeans. His hands were lazily holding on to his pockets, this close to hooking them with his thumbs. Dude looked pleased as punch to see me. By which I mean, you could tell him and Lee had a little argument about whether or not she should go all the way to Alberta to get me.

I stayed back with Poppy while Lee did a jogging walk to her Dad. He hugged her. I had a phantom feeling in response, an arm around my shoulder. It took me a sec to realize it was Poppy's, and that she was standing on her tiptoes to reach me.

"Come on," I said. "We should go say hi."

"Hunter." Mr. McKenzie took my hand to shake it. My hand did not make the effort. "And this is Poppy?" Lee had prepared him. He took Poppy's hand and shook it firmly. Her grip was a lot stronger than my wet noodle in his hand. "I'm Lee's dad," he said. "Bruce McKenzie."

"Hey," Poppy said, taking her hand back. I accidentally beamed out a smile at her.

Mr. McKenzie took us to his car, small and white and expensive. I sat in the backseat with Poppy. I was more out of place and uncomfortable than she was. I'd been away so long but nothing had changed. Not Victoria, not Lee, not her family.

Had I?

"I can drop you off at your house. Your parents should know you're here."

"They know," I said. "We can just go to the hospital."

He turned on his right signal light and turned at the next stop sign. He put on a talk-radio channel and it was the only talking going on in the car.

The streets were winding and lined with trees. It was weird to miss the prairies. I got a few glimpses of the ocean, sitting over on the right. There was nothing stopping it from going on forever.

Mr. McKenzie dropped me and Poppy off at the hospital. It was the first time I wondered what I was going to do with her. I hadn't thought this far ahead, to what would happen to her when I had to go in.

Lee stayed in the car, lifting her hand in a goodbye. She rolled down her window.

"Call me after," she said. "Don't you dare forget to call me, Hunter Ryan."

I leaned in through the open window, wanting to give her a kiss.

"Don't even think about it," Mr. McKenzie said.

I squeezed Lee's hand and said, "Come on, Pops. Let's go."

Last time I had been to this hospital, there was a chance I wouldn't make it out. We went past the wall me and Josh had sat on, him with his joint, me with my ass sticking out through the back of my hospital gown. The cafeteria on the main floor. I went straight to the elevators, jabbing at a button with my index finger.

"Hey," Poppy said, "are you going to throw up or something?"

"No," I said. I was white-knuckling the metal bar that skirted around the inside of the elevator. Poppy was fishing. Why were we here? I gave her a weak smile. "Before I moved to Lethbridge, I was in here," I told her.

"What for? Did you break a leg or something?"

"Nah," I said, shaking out my legs to show her it was nothing like that. "It was a little more serious." Inside my chest, my lungs were getting all tight. "I took some pills. Overdosed. Ended up in here."

"On purpose?"

Penner had asked me the same thing. Mom, Dad, and Bridge. Maybe I hadn't been sure before, or maybe I just liked giving them a half-answer. Poppy didn't deserve a half-answer.

"Yeah," I said.

"So what are you doing here now?"

Poppy was looking right at me. Her eyebrows were close together. That little frown line in the middle.

"Happened to my friend," I said. "Similar kind of thing. Only . . . he's still in here."

The elevator doors opened. I walked stiff-legged down the hall.

Poppy caught up to me. I felt her hand on mine. Her backpack was bouncing, the straps loose on her shoulders. Maybe I had loosened them with mine. We stopped outside Niall's room.

"Can you wait out here?" I asked her. "Just for a minute."

Poppy reached around me. Her ear pressed into my shoulder. We stayed like that for a long time. I didn't want to let her go. She was the most familiar thing about all of this: the bus ride, the hospital, the city. I took a deep breath and stepped away.

I shoved my hands into my pockets, but then I remembered I needed one of them to knock on the doorframe. I forgot to turn around to give Poppy one more smile.

Niall was lying on the hospital bed. He was a skinny body covered by a white sheet. Small machines were blinking and buzzing around him. A tube ran into his mouth. Other things in his arms and nose. He did not look like a real person. He sure didn't look like himself.

We studied Ancient Egypt in Social Studies when I was in elementary school. Me and Lee built a pyramid out of sugar cubes after we watched a couple of characters do it on an after-school special. I remember a video about these mummies being brought out of the pyramids, all skinny and shriveled. That was the first thing I thought of when I saw Niall, the almost-anniversary of his one year in the hospital and his body getting smaller.

Niall's parents were already looking at me, dressed cool and together. More together about this than I was. Niall's dad was by the window, adjusting the blinds. Like Niall could tell whether he was getting slanted light or full-on sun. They knew who I was. Niall's friend, the person who had pulled him out of the ocean to this place.

"How is he?" I asked, my voice a croak.

Niall's dad pulled on the blinds, his knuckles white from clasping the string.

"He's coming off of life support," he said.

Niall's mom looked at the floor. Her face crumpled like a paper ball. A dozen tiny wrinkles spider-webbing across her face.

"When?"

"Tomorrow."

My chest pulled tight, collapsing with the realization that this would be the last time I'd see him. For the first time, I didn't know what I'd do when this was over. I didn't know where I'd go when he was gone.

I stayed in his room, his parents flanking me beside his bed like a couple of bodyguards, for fifteen minutes. Niall was like the live wire I didn't want to touch. But there was nothing live about him. Nothing close to the Niall I knew.

I hadn't touched him since I'd pulled him out of the ocean and heaved his unconscious body into the boat. I reached out my hand, inching it closer to Niall's. The back was rough and puckered with scabs from where the IV had been passed in and out. I touched him on the back of his wrist. His skin felt wrong. It was transparent, too close to the things underneath. And scarred.

You couldn't guess his height, not by looking at him now. No one would say that he was as tall as a tree, even though that was the first thing you would have said before. His hair was cut back, just shy of being buzzed.

"Hey, Niall." My voice sounded stupid, too loud in that little room with his parents. But I went on anyway.

"I'm sorry," I told him. "I'm sorry I didn't know what you were really doing, going so far out on the ocean. I should've known. We never should've gone out. I never should've let you go so far out."

Even though I knew he wouldn't answer, there was still a part of me that hoped he would. He was almost where he'd wanted to be all along. Not hooked up to a room full of machines, but in a quiet, silent place.

I squeezed his hand.

"Bye, Niall," I said.

My chest pulled my heart back into my chest, becoming a vacuum. It squeezed so hard that it hurt. A big black hole between my lungs.

I didn't ask Niall's parents about the funeral. I could only handle saying goodbye to him once, and it felt like enough to do it in person, where he had more of a chance of hearing and knowing that I was there than he would if he was on his way underground.

With the feeling of Niall's papery skin still on my hands, I walked out of the room into the hallway.

Poppy wasn't there.

I talked to a nurse, blonde hair, blue eyes. "Hey, did you see a girl wandering around?"

She tilted her head to the side, as if she was trying to remember. "No." She put a call for Poppy over the hospital intercom.

"Poppy Haynes, please come to the registration desk. Poppy Haynes."

The receptionist in the front atrium thought she had seen Poppy.

She lifted herself out of her wheelie chair and it skitted off behind her. She peered around the atrium, eyes squinting hard. "She looked a little lost. Is she your sister?"

"Yes," I lied, knowing it was a good one.

"She might have gone out there," the receptionist said.

My heart flip-flopped and then calmed. Poppy wouldn't go far. She seemed tough as nails but there was something fragile about her, too.

Outside, it had started snowing, the sun collapsing into a sliver. The cold air from the ocean had moved in. The flakes fell through the air. It was almost as if we'd brought the weather from Alberta, carrying it all the way through the mountains and across the ocean to Victoria.

I found Poppy sitting on Josh's wall. Low to the ground but high enough that her feet didn't touch. I sat down beside her. Her permanent backpack gave her a hump, the look of a camel in the desert. I patted her on it. A way of saying she did good.

"Hey," I said.

"Hey. How was your friend?"

"Not so good," I told her. "They're taking him off life support. This was kind of goodbye."

Poppy swung her feet. Her heels glanced off the wall, the stacked bricks propelling them forward. Her hands were clasped together, making me feel the opposite of okay. She held them fingernails first, half moons sinking into her skin.

"Poppy," I said, thinking it was now or never. "I shouldn't have opened that box. That was private. It was really stupid of me to go through your stuff."

Poppy measured out her words. "What did you see?" she asked.

It wasn't the question I'd been expecting. It curve-balled toward me, making me wobble off balance.

"Some stuff about your dad."

"What stuff?" she asked. She was working over her hands, covering them all over with half moons. It had to hurt. Shoving the tips of her fingernails into her skin. I put my palm on top of her clasped hands to stop it.

"Jesus, Pops, you know what I saw. Your dad stole all that money. That's why he left, right? That's why everyone's pretty shitty to you and your mom. It's probably the reason you're homeschooled."

"*Bzzzz*," she said, an approximation of the call that sent me down to the high school office. "Wrong."

"It's what I saw."

"*Bzzzz.*" She made the sound again and tossed off my palm. She was a machine gun, shooting down my answers. "My dad didn't leave."

"So, what, he's still in town? You see him sometimes?"

Poppy's eyes, when she dragged them up from the ground to look at me, were bright.

Hunter, how could you be so stupid?

"He didn't walk out on us," Poppy said. "He jumped."

I almost laughed. I was this close. He jumped. It sounded like: Ha-ha, joke's on you, Hunter Ryan.

"Off the bridge," Poppy said. Her feet were swinging. It was so little-kid, I couldn't handle it. Her dad had jumped off a bridge and I had almost laughed. What kind of reaction was that?

That high-level bridge me and Aunt Lynne were always driving by. The bridge, the bridge, the bridge. That must have been the one he jumped off. And she never said a thing. And Aunt Lynne didn't give me a clue about what had happened to Poppy's family. I never would've guessed.

"So . . ." Poppy cocked her eyebrow at me. "I guess we have something in common." It was like she was trying to make it into a joke. But her eyes were so shiny and bright. This close to crying.

"It was pretty bad for you guys after the money thing?"

Poppy nodded. "Especially for dad. He couldn't stay."

"When did you stop going to school?"

Poppy let out a horse snort. "After those girls broke my arm."

That trio of teens who pointed me in the right direction—

where to score some weed—had done it. Those two girls with her dad's jacket. Clean break, snapped her arm. Poppy told me the story while she swung her feet on the wall.

Two weeks after Poppy's dad jumped, they cornered her at school. They took what people were saying about her and got her back for it. They came after her because they couldn't go after him.

"I puked," Poppy said.

"*Exorcist*-style?" I asked. There I went. Trying to make it a joke, just like she was. When, really, it was devastating as hell.

"They pushed me down into it. I got throw-up all over my favorite jeans."

"Jesus."

After a minute, she said, "It should've been me and my mom up there."

"Poppy, no."

"All three of us, lined up on the rails, holding hands and jumping together. Dad jumped all alone."

"Shit, Poppy. No one told me. I didn't know."

My breathing was so loud, a *hhehh hehhh hehhh* that was louder than life. I was like Lee and her asthma. My heartbeat was in my head, and it was in my chest and my left arm.

"They hated him so much," she said. "Now they hate us."

"They don't know you," I told her.

I didn't know if she believed me but I hoped she believed me enough.

"Are you coming back?" Poppy asked me.

"I don't know," I said.

"I want to go back home," she said. Her body was shaking. Just vibrating away.

I knew she had to go back, but part of me wanted her to stay. Because I think a small part of me knew that *I* might stay.

"I know. Come to my house first. We'll figure out how to get you home after."

Poppy nodded. I helped her off the wall. I wrapped her up in a hug, like she had done for me in the hospital. She was an earthquake, making my shoulders shake up and down.

We took a cab to my place. Poppy shadowed me through the front door and hung back when I saw my parents for the first time in three months. Mom and Dad rushed toward me, almost bulldozing me off my feet.

"Hunter," Mom said. "You're home."

Mom hugged me tight. Dad ruffled my hair, putting his arms around me when Mom finally relinquished her hold on me. Maybe shipping me off had been an off-the-cuff decision, something made in the moment and hard to take back.

I backed up to introduce them to Poppy, who was trying to make herself invisible in the living room. Mom and Dad were real champs about her. Mom called Mrs. Haynes in Lethbridge, only handing Poppy the phone after she'd explained everything that had happened. Dad took her into the kitchen and, a couple of minutes later, there was that telltale smell of bacon in the air.

"Have you talked to Aunt Lynne?" I asked Mom.

"I called her as soon as we heard from you this morning."

"Did she know I came back?"

Mom nodded. "She knew."

"And Poppy's mom?"

Mom squeezed my arm.

What if her and Dad had been like this when I came home from the hospital last summer? Talking to me, caring about me, giving out easy hugs. I might not have needed Lethbridge at all.

"Hunter," Mom said, "Poppy's mom called the police. Lynne calmed her down but she's still pretty worried. There's a ticket waiting for Poppy at the Greyhound station. The bus leaves this evening."

"She can't go back by herself," I said. "Not all that way."

"Her mom will meet her in Vancouver. They'll fly back to Alberta together from there."

"Oh," I said.

Poppy's mom must hate me. Police, bus rides, plane trips. All because of me.

"Are you staying?" Mom asked me. She had her hand on my arm, like she'd pull me right back if I tried to leave again.

"I don't know," I said.

We joined Dad in the kitchen. I watched him turn a couple of over-easy eggs, the fat yellow yolks perfect circles. Poppy fit in here just as easily as I had fit in at her house.

Lee came over just as we were sitting down, joining in on the afternoon brunch spread across the table. She had showered, her hair still wet. Dad slid an egg onto her plate and she built a bacon fort around it.

"So, Poppy," Lee said, "you finally get to see where Hunter's from."

"I like it," she said. She looked at me over her glass of orange juice. "It seems like a good place to stay."

I ate my eggs and left my family in the kitchen, all of them making the good kind of small talk. I went up to my bedroom for the first time since I'd left it.

My bed was made tight, all of the edges tucked under. The blinds were open. I could see the backyard through my window. It had started snowing, more sleet than anything. It was pretty white out there. The only sign that anyone had been in my room was a crease in the center of my bed, like someone had sat down right there.

I crossed the room to my closet and reached for a duffel. I was on autopilot, going through my drawers and taking out clothes I had left behind the first time. I stuffed them into the bag, not worrying about folding them or making them look neat. My hand hovered over a framed picture propped up on my dresser. The four of us, Mom, Dad, me, and Bridget, sitting on the couch a couple of Christmases ago. I don't remember who took it. It could have been Aunt Lynne, when we were all together for Christmas dinner. It was a candid shot, not really posed, but we were all looking up at the camera and it was a miracle there was no red eye. It was similar to the one Poppy kept in her book, the family portrait in miniature, taken on a random sunny day.

I almost shoved it in the duffel bag. I might have. But then I heard Lee's voice mix in with my mom and dad's, all of them talking together in the kitchen. Poppy chimed in, her twelve-year-old way of talking carrying up the stairs. It sounded like home.

I stopped filling the duffel.

I sat in the center of my bed, right in the middle of that crease. It was all catching up with me. Niall, the bus ride, home. I closed my eyes and leaned back.

"Hunter?" Poppy knocked on the doorframe, inching into my room.

"Yeah, Pops?"

"You staying?"

I bobbed my head. "I think I'm staying."

"I thought so," she said. "I have to go home. Your dad's driving me to the bus station in a sec."

"You talk to your mom?"

"I think I'm grounded," she said, smiling.

"Grounded *and* homeschooled," I said. "What a combo."

"Well," she said. "Maybe not homeschooled anymore. I might go back to school. I've been thinking about it."

"Me, too," I said. "Gotta graduate sometime."

Poppy looked around my room, taking in the surroundings. I saw her linger on that family photo. Then she blinked and nodded her head at the door.

"Come on," she said.

"I wish I could take the bus back with you," I said, following her down the stairs.

"Nah," she said. "I'm not even going all the way back. Save your bus trip for when you come to visit."

I grinned at her. "Sounds like a plan."

Dad loaded me and Poppy in the car and drove us to the bus station. The snow fell thick and heavy, the windshield wipers working overtime. Me and Poppy got out of the car at the station and went inside. Poppy was always flickering in front of me, reminding me of a hologram. Young and old all at once. Tall and short. Kid and teen. I straightened the straps of her backpack. We stood off to the side of her bus, trying to figure out how to say our version of a goodbye.

"Was it what you thought it would be?" Poppy asked me.

"No," I said, thinking of Niall. A small part of me had hoped for a movie ending. That I would sit down beside his bed and say the right words, something like a magic spell or an incantation that would wake him back up. "And, Poppy, I'm so sorry about your dad."

"Don't be."

"It's just an expression," I said. "Means I feel you."

"Well, I feel you, too," she said, "even though that sounds kind of pervy."

The line was tapering. Three more people before it was Poppy's turn.

"I'll see you again," I told her. "I should be here for Christmas. But I'm not done with Lethbridge."

"What if it's done with you?"

I cracked a smile. "It's not."

I put my arms around her before she could stop me, or change her mind, or get on the bus. There was nothing bird-boned about her. She was someone to hold onto, tight as I needed.

"Bye, Hunter," Poppy said.

She kissed me on the cheek. Soft as a feather and then she was gone.

Back in Dad's car, I watched the snow through the windshield. I ruffled my hair, making it stick on end. I was rough with it. It felt good to get in there and massage my head.

"Is she going to be okay?" Dad asked.

"Yeah," I said. "She's going to be fine."

His voice quieter, he said, "What about you?"

I turned the radio on and let it fill up the silence.

When we got home, Mom was out front, shoveling the driveway. The air smelled like snow, cool and cold and icy. The clouds had rolled in, dropping snow all over the place. But right then, there was a sliver of sun sliding through the clouds.

Me and Dad grabbed a pair of shovels from the garage and helped her with the rest of the driveway. It was just the *scrape scrape* of shovel, snow, and cement.

"Okay, Hunter?" Mom asked me.

"Yeah," I said. "I'm okay."

I tossed the snow over my shoulder and knew that, for now, I was in the right place.

ACKNOWLEDGMENTS

This book could not have been written without the thoughtful support and friendship of so many people. First, to my editor Kathy Stinson, who consistently asks the kinds of questions that challenge me to make my writing better. I am so fortunate and grateful to have such a gifted editor and author working with me! To Peter Carver and Richard Dionne at Red Deer Press for their kind emails, guidance, and support from the beginning to the end of my work on *Swimmers*. To the amazing advocates of children's and young adult literature in Lethbridge: Richard Chase, Kari Tanaka, Becky Colbeck, Leona King, Michael Pollard, Robert Runte, Ruth McMahon, and Margaret Rodermond. To Franny Stephan, for letting me share an apartment in Boston for six months, where much of *Swimmers* was imagined. To Kerrie Waddington and Caitlin Tighe for their friendship, book talking, and *My So-Called Life*. Finally, to my family: my mom, dad, and my sister Erin (and Finn!). Thank you so much for everything you've done to encourage reading and writing, and for being the first readers of all my writing.

Photo credit: Erin Bright

An Interview with
the Author

1. Readers are always curious to know where writers get their ideas. Where did you get the idea to write *Swimmers*?

I wrote a short story called "Look at it This Way" a few years ago, about a teenage boy who is asked by his psychologist to write four letters to a recipient that he chooses. The letters are addressed to a woman named Mrs. Shipman, whose daughter was killed in a car crash by the protagonist's older brother. His brother goes to jail and the protagonist has to deal with the aftermath. The short story, being a short story, was not very long (I'd really like to return to that short story again and turn it into a much longer book) and, when it was finished, I realized that I missed writing about the relationship between a teenager and his psychologist, as well as writing about a teenager trying to deal with the repercussions on his life of someone else's actions. Hunter and *Swimmers* came out of those ideas—how to deal with what his best friend Niall has done, and how he has a chance to work that out with Mr. Penner in weekly meetings in the high school office.

2. The main character of *Swimmers* is a 17-year-old male, and this is not the first time you've written from an adolescent male perspective. Did you find any particular challenges to getting inside Hunter's head that were different, say, from getting inside the head of your female protagonists?

Some of my favorite male characters in YA books were written by female writers, like Cameron in Libba Bray's *Going Bovine*. Conversely, some of my favorite female characters were written by male writers, such as Cait in Kevin Brooks's *Lucas*, Lyra in Phillip Pullman's *The Golden Compass*, and Tiffany Aching in Terry Pratchett's *The Wee Free Men*. Even though there are definitely differences between female and male characters, I think there's a lot about being a teenager that is fairly universal. I think in terms of identity, self-consciousness, loneliness, that feeling of invincibility, and elation, all teenagers have some experience and understanding. I think more than trying to write a female or a male character, I was trying to write more about these things, and what it's like to be a teenager who is going through these things. I don't think I went into writing this story too worried about writing a male rather than a female character. Hunter was the best character to tell this story.

3. Hunter is a compelling character, but some of the secondary characters in *Swimmers* are also pretty interesting people. Was there a character in *Swimmers* you found yourself rooting for especially, someone whose story you really hoped would have a happy ending?

Bridget and Hunter's Aunt Lynne were two of my favorite characters to write, and I think I imagined much more background material for the two of them than almost any other character. I love writing about siblings and sibling relationships and, initially I wanted Bridget to play a much bigger role in the story. In an early, early, early draft, Bridget was actually the main character of the story, and she was watching her brother Hunter deal with what had happened to Niall. That draft didn't make it very far, because I think it was always Hunter's story, first and foremost, and he had to be central to it. But I liked Bridget as the older sister who was there for her brother, even when he didn't want her to be, and trying to figure out her own life, and leaving home when so much of it was with her parents and Hunter in Victoria.

I felt a similar way about Hunter's Aunt Lynne, in that I was really interested in what her life looked like before, after, and during the time that Hunter had come to stay with her. I kind of felt that she would have loved the opportunity to have her nephew come to live with her for a few months, and I liked that idea that she had room in her life for him.

I felt like it would have changed her just as much as it changed him.

4. How important do you think happy endings are, or aren't, in books for young people?

This question makes me think of a throwaway line in the movie *Silver Linings Playbook*, where the main character Pat finishes Ernest Hemingway's *A Farewell to Arms* by saying: "He survives the war after getting blown up. He survives it and he escapes to Switzerland with Catherine. You think he ends it there? No! She dies, Dad! I mean, the world's hard enough as it is, guys. Can't someone say, Hey, let's be positive? Let's have a good ending to the story?" I love happy endings in young adult books. It's a unique type of ending, because the ending to a young adult novel is never a solid ending to what happens to the teenage characters. Young adulthood is so much about moving on, toward adulthood and away from childhood, that endings aren't permanent and stable. So when they're happy, it's like a bit of optimism for what happens next in their lives.

That being said, I also think that unhappy, sad, or ambiguous readings are so important for teenagers to read as well. Books that aren't wrapped up perfectly at the end, and are, instead, ambiguous and unstable, can also teach teenagers that they aren't alone, reflecting a more bleak reality that might be closer to their own lives. That happy ending doesn't always reflect a teenage reader's own version of reality, and might not seem as genuine as something much bleaker. Especially in high school English classes (where books like *Wuthering Heights*, *Hamlet*, *Macbeth*, and others with their doom-and-gloom endings seem to always be on the reading lists), I think it's so important to have a mix of happy ending and not-so-happy ending books, in order to really reflect the reality of teenage readers and their understanding of how stories and endings happen. It can be hard to handle the unhappy ending.

5. What was your favorite scene in *Swimmers* to write?

There are a couple of party scenes in *Swimmers* and, though both of them were really fun to write, one sort of stands out more than the other. The exchanges between Lee and Hunter were probably my favorite to write (outside of the ones between Hunter and his psychologist), and you really get to see them throughout all stages of a relationship. And my favorite part of their relationship happens at a party near the beginning of the book. I remember reading a book by Jaclyn Moriarty when I was younger, where a group of teenagers from Ashbury High School get locked in a walk-in closet for the night, and what happens inside of the closet is told from about three or four points of view. My favorite scene to write was when Hunter and Lee get stuck in an attic at a house party with a bunch of other people.

6. Who would you say are your favorite writers (or

books), and how do you think they have influenced you as a writer?

I read constantly when I was younger, both adult books and young adult books. Now that I'm working on my PhD in English, which is on young adult literature, I have a built-in excuse to read YA literature. It's my job! It's for my dissertation! But really, I've always loved YA books and the authors that write them. I absolutely love Australian writer Jaclyn Moriarty and her Ashbury/Brookfield series, Libba Bray for *Going Bovine* and The Diviners series, Terry Pratchett's Tiffany Aching books, *The Coldest Girl in Coldtown* by Holly Black, and the steampunk/paranormal/ romance series (there's an adult one and a YA one) by Gail Carriger. I've really loved being able to read YA books by authors like Moriarty and Bray as a teenager, and then their newer publications as an adult. I think reading constantly has been the biggest influence on me as a writer, and reading YA books about teenage characters, both as a teenager and as an adult. It's so neat to watch the way stories for teenagers change, and then write along with other authors.

TV probably also plays a big part in influencing my writing because I watch a lot of it. The stories being told on TV are so good, complicated, and appeal to teenagers just as much as YA lit does. And then I'm really influenced by trashy reality shows and WWE, which might not show up too much in Swimmers, but it definitely formed the background noise of much of the drafting process.

7. Who do you see as the "swimmers" in this book?

I saw Poppy and Hunter as the "swimmers" in this book. And oh, man, swimming can be hard. If you haven't done it for a while and then you jump in a pool and try to swim a couple of laps? It's instant sink-to-the-bottom-of-the-pool. I'm more of a flutterboard and flippers swimmer. Also, it can be insanely disorienting and terrifying if you don't know how to swim, and no matter how hard you kick your legs or tread water, you can't do that forever. Poppy and Hunter have both been treading water for a long time. They've been working so hard to stay in one place, heads just bobbing above the water, that they haven't even worked out how to go forward yet. I saw their stories as the hardest work ever, both of them having to relearn how to work at their normal lives and find a way to flail themselves forward toward that. Maybe swimming's like riding a bicycle—you never forget how to do it—but it still takes a long time to get good at it again.

9-16-14